A LOVE STORY IN THE TIME OF THE GREAT WAR

A Novel

By

Sandra Gowing

Published by:
Wildebeest Publishing Company, LLC
Syracuse, New York

Wildebeest Publishing Company, LLC
6456 Collamer Road
Syracuse, NY 13057

For more information about copyrights and usage, special discounts on bulk purchases, workshops, and engagements, please contact Wildebeest Publishing Company, LLC at (315) 220-0217, info@wildebeestpublishing.com, or online at www.wildebeestpublishing.com

Wildebeest Publishing Company, LLC paperback First Edition [September 2024], United States of America

Photographs property of Sandra Gowing

ISBN: 978-1-958233-31-3 (paperback)
LLCN 2024918121

For Doris and Philip
The lives that ended too soon
will live on forever
through the pages of this book

TABLE OF CONTENTS

PART I
LOVE

CHAPTER 1

Philip had heard the train whistle earlier, so he knew it had arrived at the station, even though he wasn't yet able to see it. He marched in cadence with the rest of his company, his sergeant's deep voice ringing out in his ears – "One, two, three, four." As he marched, he felt the heavy weight of his pack on his back. The pack contained all his belongings and would be with him for the next several months.

He heard the sound of the train's engine and smelled its smoke before he could actually see it. When it finally came into view, it appeared small at first, becoming larger and larger as he moved closer, finally becoming a huge, hulking presence hovering on the track as it lay in wait.

It was a gray, overcast day, unseasonably cold, with a biting wind that took away his breath and penetrated the fabric of his uniform trousers. He looked over at the small crowd of well-wishers standing on the platform. The flags that some of them carried flapped and whipped around in the wind.

I wonder if Doris is here, he thought.

He had discouraged his wife from coming to see him off due to the cold weather. He hated to think of her standing out in it but couldn't help hoping she would be there.

"I want to be there," she had insisted. "My father will drive me in his motorcar. Look for me. I'll be wearing my red hat."

His eyes scanned the crowd, and he saw a flash of red. He smiled as he saw her standing next to her father, vigorously waving her arm. He continued to march to the train, and as he started to turn toward the entrance, their eyes met, and she blew him a kiss. Just before he climbed the steps onto the train, he turned back slightly and lifted his arm to wave, but someone had moved in front of Doris, and he could no longer see her.

Doris stood on the platform next to her father, watching as Philip disappeared into the train. A small woman, she continued to stand in the bitter wind, staring at the train until it finally started to move slowly down the tracks toward Hoboken, New Jersey and the ship that would carry the men to France. It was November 20, 1917, and a war was raging in Europe. The men on the train would soon become part of it.

Doris stood and watched the train until it was out of sight. Then, she and her father turned and headed back to the other end of the platform where the Ford Model T was parked. She shivered with the cold and reached up and pulled the collar of her coat more closely around her neck. She stumbled along, her eyes blurred by tears she was trying to hold back. Her father, unsure how to comfort her, finally reached across her back and lightly patted her shoulder.

"He'll be back," he said.

Doris nodded, lost in thought, as they continued to walk. The sky suddenly appeared brighter, and Doris squinted as she looked up and saw that the dark clouds that had been dominating the sky had briefly parted, allowing an interval of bright sunshine.

As she felt the warm sun on her face, she had a fleeting memory of the day, just six months ago, when she had first met Philip at a movie house in downtown Syracuse, New York. She remembered so clearly leaving the darkened theater and stepping out into the bright sunshine with Philip following closely behind.

Their story began on one of the last days of the school year, a beautiful late spring day. Doris and her best friend, Helen Shore, had decided to leave school after lunch.

"Let's skip our last classes and go to the movies," Doris had said.

Helen, being the more serious student, had been hesitant at first, but Doris had talked her into it, saying, "It's almost the end of the year. They probably won't even miss us."

When Helen finally agreed, they had taken a bus downtown. They got off the bus on Salina Street and headed for a nearby movie house. There were some men in uniforms on the street, and Doris pointed to them, saying, "They must be from the new recruit camp out at the fairgrounds."

As Doris and Helen approached the theater's box office they noticed two of the uniformed men were standing in line. The girls stepped up behind them. The men turned and looked at them and Doris, thinking how handsome they both were, smiled what she considered to be her most captivating smile.

The two girls bought their tickets, and as they entered the theater, Doris said, "Did you see them looking at us?"

"Yes, I did," Helen said with a muffled giggle.

The girls stood in the back of the theater, waiting for their eyes to adjust to the darkness. The movie was already in progress as they stood looking over the seats, many of which were empty.

Doris whispered, "Look, there's those two soldiers. Let's sit next to them."

"Wouldn't that be kind of forward?" Helen asked, but Doris couldn't tell if that was an excited or apprehensive response, and Doris was already entering the row where the two men were seated. Helen reluctantly followed, and as they took the seats next to them, both men turned and looked at the girls, eliciting another bright smile from Doris. The lights came on at the end of the film and people started to leave, but the two soldiers remained in their seats.

Doris said to Helen, "Let's stay and watch the part we missed."

"Okay, good idea."

Doris turned to the man sitting next to her and asked, "Are you guys from the recruit camp?"

Somewhat startled, the young man turned toward her and answered, "Yes, they gave us the afternoon off."

The man next to him leaned across and said, "My name is Andy Wise, and this is my buddy, Philip Boughton."

"I'm Doris Bowman, and this is my friend, Helen Shore."

"Do you girls work downtown?"

"The girls both laughed, and Doris said, "We decided to skip school this afternoon and go to the movies."

"So, you're school girls," Andy said.

Doris said, "Yes, but we're graduating next month. I'm almost eighteen."

The lights went out, and the film started up again. When it reached the point where it had been earlier when they had come in, the four got up from their seats and made their way outside. It was a warm day, and they stood near the theater entrance and talked. Andy pulled out a package of cigarettes and offered them around. The men each took one, and although Helen declined, Doris accepted one. After Andy lit it for her, she took a deep drag. She wasn't a regular smoker, but a neighborhood boy had once shown her how, and she now wanted to appear grown up. The other three watched her as she coughed at first but then took several more drags before dropping the cigarette on the ground and grinding it out with her foot. The four stood talking until Helen said, "We should go. My mother will wonder where I am," and they started up the block toward the streetcar stop.

A gust of cold wind and the return of the dark clouds quickly brought Doris back to the present moment and the reality that she was no longer a carefree schoolgirl. She was now a married woman with a baby on the way and a husband who was going off to a faraway country to fight and maybe die for a cause she knew little about.

Well, that can't happen, she thought. *He can't die. He will come back. He has to.*

As the four young people walked away from the theater toward the streetcar stop on that warm spring afternoon, they paired off with Doris walking beside Philip and Helen with Andy. As they walked, they talked.

Doris asked, "Are you guys from around here?"

"Well, Andy is. He's from Liverpool, but I'm from Michigan."

"Michigan," Doris tried to remember her geography. "Is that far from here?"

"About 500 miles."

"What's it like there?"

"Well, it looks a lot like it does around here, but I lived on a farm before I went to college."

"You were in college?"

"Yes, business college."

"Why did you join the Army?"

"A recruiter came to our school and gave a talk about the war and how it was our duty to serve our country. A lot of my friends were joining up. It just seemed like the right thing to do."

They reached the stop, looked down the street, and saw the Elmwood streetcar in the distance. "That's ours," Doris said. They turned and looked at each other, and as their eyes met, everything in the background seemed to fade away, as if they were the only two people in the world. Time seemed to stop as both felt something neither had experienced in the past. Was that the moment that they fell in love? No one could ever know, but they were both aware of something special happening.

Philip said, "I wish I could see you again."

"Well, maybe we could meet somewhere, like the movies again."

"The problem is, I'm not sure when I can get another pass to leave the camp."

"You could call me. I have a telephone. Is there one at the camp?"

"Yes, I'm sure there's one in the office. I'd have to have permission to use it, but our sergeant is an okay guy, and I think if I ask him, he'll let me."

"My number is 5768."

Philip felt in his pockets and then asked Andy, "Do you have a pencil?"

"No."

"Well, I think I can remember it. I have a good memory. 5768. It's an easy number to remember, 5768." He repeated it several times before saying goodbye as the two girls boarded the streetcar.

CHAPTER 2

Once inside the streetcar and having taken seats, the girls waved to the men as the car moved down the street. Helen turned to Doris and asked, "What was Philip like?"

"Well, he's from a farm in Michigan. He seemed really nice. I liked him."

"You gave him your telephone number. What will your mother say if he calls?"

"I don't know." Both girls were from rather straight-laced, protective families. Receiving a telephone call from a boy her own age who attended her school or church was one thing, but one from a soldier who was a complete stranger would be quite another.

Helen asked Doris, "What if he asks you to go out on a date? Would you go?"

"Maybe." Then, "Yes."

Helen looked at Doris with raised eyebrows, and both girls laughed. They both had a healthy interest in the opposite sex. They attended parties and dances with boys their age and there had been furtive kisses in dim corners away from the eyes of chaperones, but neither was accustomed to going out alone with boys. Although "dating" was becoming more popular among young people, it had yet to catch on among their circle of friends, and their parents were somewhat old-fashioned.

Helen asked, "Would your parents let you?"

"I don't know, but I'm almost 18."

Doris was born in 1899 in the Finger Lakes village of Aurora, the first child of Horace and Louise Bowman. A few months after her birth, the family moved to Syracuse, where Horace took a job as a park caretaker.

Elmwood Park was a scenic park on the southwest side of Syracuse. It had a brook running through it and several walking paths. The park was at the end of a streetcar line, and an entrance fee was charged. It had opened several years ago as the area's only temperance park and offered various kinds of amenities. The brook was dammed, and a small lake resulted. There were amusements such as a merry-go-round and swan boats, as well as concession stands, picnic shelters, a band concert stand, and games such as horseshoes and badminton.

The Bowman family had a small house on the grounds, and they enjoyed living there. Louise liked walking on the paths with Doris in her carriage, and when Horace had an afternoon off, the family would take rides on the swan boats, enjoy a picnic, or attend a band concert.

Things were fine until 1902, when the ownership of the park changed. A dance hall was opened, and there was talk of a liquor license. It was now attracting a lot of ruffians, and there was often drinking and gambling.

One day, Louise said to Horace, "I don't feel safe here anymore."

Horace agreed and said, "No, I don't feel it's a good place for my family. I'm going to look for another job."

Horace found other employment, and the family rented a house in the nearby neighborhood. Over the next several years, Horace worked for a number of local companies, and the family lived in different places around the Elmwood and Valley neighborhoods. Things were not always easy for them. Horace sometimes lost a job and then had to take a lower-paying one, making it necessary for them to find cheaper housing and forcing them to move often. Horace sometimes had to work more than one job, and Louise helped out by sewing for people.

The Bowmans had hoped for more children, but none had been forthcoming. They adored their only daughter and wanted the best for her. They somehow found the money for Doris to take dance and piano lessons. The Bowmans didn't have a piano, but Louise's mother, Jennie Bogardus, did. Jennie lived nearby and made sure Doris practiced on her piano.

Doris had always been a spirited child, or as her grandmother liked to call her, a little rascal. She, along with a group of neighborhood children, tended to become involved in various kinds of mischief, snatching cooling baked goods from window sills, and knocking on doors then running off. They tramped through gardens, sometimes knocking over flower pots and picking vegetables and fruit and then pelting them at the sides of houses and cars. They had gotten in trouble for breaking windows and once had even started a neighbor's motorcar and managed to drive it off down the street, running it into a field before it stalled out. They loved playing pranks and had once removed sheets from a clothesline and ran to St. Agnes cemetery, where they proceeded to drape the sheets over the statues, giving them the appearance of ghosts. It sometimes seemed to Louise that every day, an irate neighbor would appear at her door complaining of some misbehavior, making it necessary to punish Doris.

However, no amount of punishment seemed to change things, and this behavior continued for several years, causing the Bowmans a great deal of frustration. Things finally came to a head in 1913 when Doris was picked up by the authorities and taken to juvenile headquarters. She had fallen in with a crowd of older children who were causing trouble in the neighborhood, motivating a neighbor to report them to the police, saying they were unsupervised and "running wild." Doris was accused of associating with "persons of immoral behavior," and Horace was called and had to make an appearance in court. Doris was given a suspended sentence, and Horace was admonished for not giving her better supervision. She was assigned to a probation officer, a caring woman who gave her a stern lecture and warned her to mend her ways lest she end up in a detention home. She was then dismissed without further punishment, but the incident had scared her enough to finally begin to turn things around.

The Bowmans were extremely distressed by all this. The incident had been reported in the local newspaper, and they feared for Doris's reputation.

Louise cried and said, "Where have we gone wrong? We try to be good parents, but it seems that there is nothing we can do to change her behavior! It just gets worse and worse!"

Horace said, "I've been so busy trying to make a living and get by that I guess I haven't paid enough attention to her. Well, things are going to change. We can't let this kind of thing happen again. From now on, we will keep a tight rein on her."

At about that time, the Bowmans were starting to do better financially. Horace had a steady job and had made some careful investments in local companies. Syracuse, at that time, was a hotbed for inventions, and there were many opportunities with both established and start-up companies. The Bowmans bought a house on Armstrong Place on St. Agnes Hill and were able to furnish it nicely and purchase a piano for Doris. A couple of years later, Horace bought a Ford Model T. Louise joined the ladies' circle at the Elmwood Presbyterian Church, where they were members.

Doris remained lively and fun-loving and continued to have a *mind of her own,* as her mother liked to say. Her parents continued to keep a *tight rein* on her, but they began to worry less. When she started high school at Valley Academy, she became friends with a nice group of girls, Helen Shore among them. Doris was pretty rather than beautiful in the classic sense. She had nice features with beautiful blue eyes, dark, wavy hair, and lovely skin. She also possessed an abundance of charm and sparkled in a way that seemed to light up any room she was in. She was popular among her friends, enjoyed going to parties, and loved to dance.

Doris was intelligent but didn't do as well as she could have in school, never spending enough time on her studies. She did enough to get by and always managed to receive a passing grade but didn't really like school, except for the social aspect. There were employment opportunities in the city for girls, and she talked of dropping out of school, getting a job, and earning her own money. Most of all, she wanted to get out from under her parents' control. The Bowmans, however, wanted very badly for her to finish high school and get her diploma. Neither of them had attended high school and felt now that their own financial position was more secure; there was no need for their daughter to quit school and go to work, as so many others had to do.

Doris wasn't sure what she would do after graduation. Women were now demanding the vote and going out into the world more. She couldn't imagine staying home with her mother and engaging in household tasks, attending teas, and doing whatever it was the ladies from their church did when they got together. She supposed she would seek some type of employment but didn't know what. Horace, being forward-thinking, had suggested she attend one of the local colleges, perhaps taking a stenography course to prepare for a career in business, but Doris had had enough of school. Louise was more traditional and had hopes of Doris meeting and marrying a nice gentleman who would provide her with a comfortable life. Doris had listened to her parents' suggestions without much comment. She had made no decisions.

Now, as she rode the streetcar back to Elmwood, Doris's mind was on Philip. *I wonder if he really will call. Maybe he'll forget all about me as soon as he gets back to his camp. For all I know, he may already have a*

girlfriend back home where he's from. He did seem to like me, though. He was so nice and so different from the boys around here. I wonder what it would be like to go out on a date with him.

She was imagining being in his embrace and was just about to be kissed by him, when Helen's voice pulled her out of her daydream. "Doris, are you listening to me?"

She had been looking out the window, but she now turned to face Helen, who was looking at her with a puzzled expression. "Oh," she said, "Sorry, I was thinking about something else. Go on with what you were saying."

Helen started talking about the upcoming graduation and the conversation continued in this way for the remainder of the ride.

CHAPTER 3

Philip and Andy crossed the street and walked to the corner where they could catch a bus back to the camp. The two men were Army privates who were stationed at nearby Camp Syracuse, where they were receiving basic training and awaiting transport to France, where they would fight in the Great War.

They had arrived at the recruit camp on the same day and were assigned adjacent beds in their eight-man tent.

Philip was new to Syracuse, having come from Michigan, but Lawrence Andrew Wise, called Andy by his friends, was a local boy whose family lived in the nearby suburb of Liverpool. Andy had taken Philip under his wing, showing him around the city when they had a day off and could get a pass, and they had become good friends.

Philip had been repeating Doris's telephone number over and over to himself. As soon as they got to the camp, he would write it down. They boarded their bus and talked about the film and the two girls they had met. Andy did most of the talking with Philip, only half listening. His mind was on Doris. He thought she was the prettiest girl he had ever seen. When their eyes met, he felt as if a charge of electricity had shot through him, and he was suddenly unable to breathe. He had never met anyone quite like her before. She seemed so carefree and full of fun. He decided he would ask his sergeant for permission to use the telephone tomorrow, and if given that permission, he would call her.

Philip had been born on a farm in south central Michigan in 1897. By the time he was thirteen, his mother, Nellie, had been widowed twice, and she and her two sons, Philip and Charles, were back living with her parents, Frank and Angeline Smith, in the family home in the town of Marshall. Philip loved his grandparents and had liked living with them, but Nellie hated it. She had become accustomed to having her own home and, in addition to that, her mother was very bossy. Angeline was forever telling Nellie what to do and this angered her, but she had no choice but to stay there, as she had no way to support herself and her sons.

The following year, Nellie met Claude Osborn, a local farmer who had never been married and was looking for a wife who would care for his home and give him children. Nellie saw marriage to Claude as an escape from her parents' home and eagerly accepted his proposal. Claude had a small family farm just outside of town, and the family moved there.

Philip hadn't wanted to move to the farm. He had liked living in town where he had friends and there were a lot of things to do but was given no choice. The house was old and rundown – not as nice as the Smiths' residence in town. The Smiths also had an indoor bathroom, whereas the farmhouse had an outdoor toilet. Philip had hated going out on cold winter mornings to use the outhouse. He thought his mother probably didn't like it much either, although she never said anything. He had also hated farm work.

The family barely managed to eke out a living on the farm by growing vegetables for their own consumption and selling what they didn't use at a market. A large plot of land was given over to growing field corn, which Claude sold to local farmers for cattle feed, buying back a portion of it to feed his own few dairy cows.

Those cows, along with several chickens, also provided food and income. An old draft horse pulled the plow and wagon, and the family raised a hog every year for meat. Philip found farm work tedious and boring at best and backbreaking at its worst. Claude Osborn was a tough taskmaster, and he and Philip argued a lot. Claude was easier on Philip's younger brother, Charlie, whom he seemed to like better.

Philip and Charlie often talked about this, Philip saying, "You don't seem to mind the work on the farm. I really hate it, but you hardly ever complain about it."

Charlie said, "I don't much like it either, but what good does it do to complain? It seems better to just do the work, and it makes it easier to get along with Claude." Charlie was an easy-going sort who always seemed to go along with things. He was one for smoothing things out when Claude came down on Philip too hard. Although he was the younger brother, he often took on the role of protector.

Charlie had bought a used violin in a second-hand shop and had found someone to teach him to play it. He seemed to have a natural talent for music and could play by ear after hearing a song. He had even been asked to play in church. He often played for the family in the evening and could even bring a smile to Claude's face.

Both boys worked long hours on the farm and often missed school. Philip managed to get his eighth-grade diploma and had hoped to go to high school, but Claude said he thought he had enough education and needed him on the farm. Angered by this, Philip did his best to do his work on the farm and get along with his stepfather, but it was often difficult. There were frequent arguments, and things finally came to a head one day, with Philip leaving the farm in anger. He asked his grandparents if he could move in with them, and they were agreeable.

Philip found a job working for a grocer on State Street. He gave his grandparents some of his pay but put the rest into savings. He worked hard at the store, cleaning and stocking shelves. His employer, Mr. Butler, found him to be hard-working and intelligent. Mr. Butler began giving him more responsibility, including having him help with his account books. Philip enjoyed this and found he had an aptitude for figures.

One day, Mr. Butler gave him some information about Michigan Business and Normal College which had a school in Battle Creek. The school required only an eighth-grade diploma for entrance and a certificate from there would qualify him to teach in a rural school or pursue a job in business. Determined to never go back to the hardscrabble life on the farm, in the summer of 1916, he applied to the school and made arrangements to attend. In late August, he moved to Battle Creek. He found a room in a boarding house and began classes.

Most of Philip's time had been taken up by his studies, but he managed to find a job cleaning classrooms to earn extra money. He liked living in Battle Creek and made new friends there. He received occasional letters from Nellie, telling him the news from home. In the fall of 1916, Philip received a letter announcing the birth of his half-brother, Glen.

Philip had gone home over the Christmas holidays. He went around to visit his former employer, Mr. Butler, and made a trip out to the farm to visit his mother and meet his new brother. He had never been especially interested in babies, but the Osborns were very happy. Claude was in an especially good mood, proud to now have a son, and the two managed to get along. Philip's father came from a large family and Philip had several girl cousins who were taking turns helping with the baby. He'd had a good visit but had been glad to leave and get back to school. Not long after that visit, he received a letter from Nellie telling him that the baby boy had died. He had suddenly become ill, and the doctor had been called. The doctor had told Nellie and Claude that Glen had an especially bad case of diphtheria, and there wasn't much he could do. The baby had died within days, and Nellie and Claude had been grief-stricken.

That year, the newspapers were full of news about the war in Europe, and Philip had followed these stories with great interest. There was increasing talk of the United States entering the war, although President Wilson had so far resisted it. Finally, on April 6, 1917, the United States entered the Great War. Many men would be needed to fight, and there was talk of a military draft, although Congress had yet to enact it.

Philip was excited about the idea of going to war and didn't want to wait to be drafted. Recruiting posters were going up everywhere and some of Philip's friends were talking of enlisting. When his school term ended at the end of April, he went to the recruiting office in Battle Creek and enlisted in the Army. Philip didn't have a middle name. When the enlistment papers required one, and the recruiter suggested he use a family name, he had thought of his stepfather, who had just lost his son. On impulse, he had said, "Osborn." For the remainder of his life, he would be known as "Philip O. Boughton."

Philip had gone home and told his family what he had done. Nellie had mixed feelings about it. She was proud of Philip but feared for his safety. *"Am I to lose another son?"* she said. The loss of her baby was still very new and raw. The thought of Philip going across the ocean to a foreign country, and the chance he could die there, was almost too much for her to bear. She had hoped to have another child but was now in her late thirties and knew there was less and less chance of that as time went by. Charlie had been proud and excited for his brother. Claude hadn't said much. In the end, the family had given its blessing, and within a short time, Philip was on a train, headed for Syracuse, New York, and recruit camp. His great adventure had begun. He couldn't wait to get over to France and start fighting the Germans. He had read and heard speeches about the glories of war and had daydreams of becoming a hero.

Now, as he rode back to the camp, these thoughts that had been at the forefront of his mind for the past month had suddenly been pushed aside and replaced with those of the girl he had just met. He smiled at the memory of her pretty face and the shapely ankles he had noticed as she boarded the streetcar. His heart skipped a beat as he imagined holding her close and kissing her. He wondered what she was doing at that minute and whether she was also thinking of him.

CHAPTER 4

Philip sat at a table in the recreation tent, trying to concentrate on the letter he was writing to his mother. The men had been given time off and had been instructed to use it to write letters home to their families. It was now June, and Philip had settled into life at Camp Syracuse. The recruits had their first call at seven AM, after which they fell into formation and marched to the mess hall for breakfast. After breakfast, they had various training activities. They attended classes, went out on the rifle range, and learned to shoot and clean their rifles. They had instructions in bayonet fighting, which involved running at large bags of sand with bayonets, and also spent time running and exercising in order to improve their physical condition.

There was a camaraderie among the men at the camp, all feeling they were in this together, and Philip had made many friends, with Andy Wise remaining his best friend. Upon meeting that first day at the camp, the two men had immediately formed a bond and whenever either of them had any kind of difficulty or problem, they tended to seek each other out.

As Philip wrote to his mother, his thoughts kept returning to the girl he had met at the movie house. He had promised to call her and had gone to his sergeant requesting permission to use the camp telephone. His sergeant was a tough but fair man who, if caught in a good mood, could usually be counted on to grant a reasonable request from a man he considered a good soldier – one who obeyed orders and did his work without complaint. Philip had received permission and placed the call to Doris, hoping she would be home. Mrs. Bowman answered the telephone, and after giving his name, Philip had asked to speak to Doris. Mrs. Bowman had then handed the telephone to Doris, and Philip's heart skipped a beat when he heard her voice. They talked for a few minutes and agreed to talk again the next time Philip had free time and could use the telephone.

Philip wrote:

Dear Mother,

Thank you for all the news from home. I'm sorry Grandpa was sick and glad he is feeling better. I hope things are going well on the farm.

Things are fine here at the camp. We are learning new things every day.

Yesterday, we learned how to clean our rifles. We go to classes every day. The classes are the school of the soldier, the school of the squad, and the school of the company. Today's class was the school of the soldier.

Sometimes, we have to work in the kitchen or do guard duty. We also go on long marches into the countryside. Sometimes, these last for three or four days, and we camp out along the way. The people from nearby towns know we are there, and they bring us pies and cakes.

We have been putting up tents for the new men coming in. I work with my friend, Andy Wise, Andy's my best friend here at the camp. He is showing me around the city, and we have gone to the movies together.

I met a very nice girl named Doris Bowman. She gave me her telephone number and I called her. She is very pretty, and I hope to see her again. I will write again soon. Tell Charlie I will write to him, too.

Your loving son,
Philip

Louise Bowman looked at her daughter as she hung up the telephone. "Who was that?" she asked.

"He's a soldier from the recruit camp."

"How did you meet him?"

Doris thought fast. "Helen introduced him to me."

Louise frowned. "How does Helen know a soldier from the recruit camp?"

"I think her mother invited him to dinner at their house," Doris said, hoping her mother wouldn't ask Mrs. Shore about it. Both families attended the same church, Elmwood Presbyterian.

Louise nodded slowly. She had heard about people doing that. Since the camp had opened, the local population had become very excited and citizens were being asked to make the soldiers feel welcome. "Take a soldier home to dinner" was a popular slogan.

Doris then said, "He's really nice. I liked him. He said he would call back. He wants to see me again."

Louise said, "Well, maybe we should invite him to dinner here." She was thinking *that I could get a look at the boy and judge his character for myself. Otherwise, she is likely to sneak off and meet him on her own. Louise also wanted to do her part for the war effort and didn't like the idea of being bested by the Shores.* She said, "When he calls back, ask him to come to Sunday dinner."

Doris could hardly believe her good fortune, but she only said, "Yes, I'll ask him the next time he calls."

When Philip called a few days later, Doris told him that her mother had invited him to dinner the following Sunday. Passes to leave the base and go into the city were usually available to men who weren't assigned to duty at that time and had a record of good conduct. For ten cents, the men could catch a bus that would take them the four miles to downtown Syracuse, where there were several movie houses and theaters that they could enjoy and where they could get on a streetcar that would take them to other parts of the city or the surrounding suburbs.

Philip received a pass and on the following Sunday, caught a bus from camp and then a streetcar to Elmwood. He arrived at Doris's house and was introduced to her parents. After a few pleasantries, they sat down to dinner.

Louise said, "I hear you had dinner with the Shores."

Philip looked puzzled. "The Shores?" he said and looked at Doris, who was nodding her head. "Um, yes," he said.

Louise started to say something, but Horace changed the subject by saying, "Well, young man, we want to hear all about what's going on at the recruit camp."

Philip said, "Well, sir, there are new men coming in every day, and tents need to be set up for them to sleep in, so we spend a lot of time doing that. We also have classes and training, learning to be soldiers. We go on long marches, trying to get in condition for when we go to France and we will have to do a lot of walking. They have also put us to work putting in telephone lines in the village of Lakeland."

Horace asked, "When do you expect to leave for France?"

"I don't know, sir. Nobody has told us when we will be leaving."

The two men then talked about the war and the fact that the British and French appeared to badly need the help of the Americans. They both expressed confidence that once the US soldiers arrived "over there," the tide would turn, and the war quickly won.

The Bowmans wanted to know about life on the farm in Michigan.

Philip said, "Well, it's a hard life." He went on to explain that it was not only the work itself that was hard but the fact that so many things were beyond one's control, the weather being just one of them. A long dry spell could mean a failed crop. Also, farm accidents were common, and a farmer who met with one or who fell ill might not be able to work his fields for weeks or months. Any of these things could lead to the incurring of debt or, even worse, the loss of a farm. Philip spoke mostly in general terms, not mentioning his disagreeable stepfather or how much he hated farm work, but he did say the life was hard on his mother. He said, "Besides her regular housework, she works in the garden and makes jam and puts up vegetables in jars for the winter. She also helps out by taking care of the animals." He said he had completed a year of business college and hoped to pursue another kind of work after he finished his military service.

Through all this, the Bowmans listened thoughtfully. They hadn't known what to expect upon meeting Philip but were pleasantly surprised. Nellie Osborn had instilled good manners in her sons, and Philip was polite and well-spoken. Initially nervous about meeting Doris's parents, Philip began to relax. Louise was a good cook, and the home-cooked meal was a pleasant change from Army fare. Philip occasionally glanced over at Doris and she smiled sweetly when their eyes met, causing a momentary fluttering in his heart.

After dinner, they retired to the parlor, and Horace said, "Doris, why don't you play the piano for us?"

Doris always enjoyed being the center of attention and was glad to oblige. She had taken piano lessons for several years and was a mediocre pianist, never having practiced as much as she should have, but there were a few pieces she could play quite well, and she played those. She made a few mistakes, sometimes striking the wrong key but Philip, knowing little about music, wasn't aware of them and enjoyed listening to her play very much.

The afternoon passed pleasantly and soon it was time for Philip to return to the camp. Before he left, he turned to Doris and said, "You like the movies, don't you?"

She said, "Oh, yes, I love them. Lillian Gish and Mary Pickford are my favorite actresses."

Philip turned to Horace and asked, "Would it be alright if I called for Doris and took her to see a film?"

Horace looked at Louise, who nodded her assent, and then he said, "Yes, that would be fine."

Doris enthusiastically accepted, and they agreed that Philip would call for her, and they would take a streetcar downtown to one of the movie houses.

Doris walked outside with Philip as he left, and as soon as they were alone, he asked, "Who are the Shores, and why did you tell your mother I had dinner with them?"

"Helen's family. Remember you met Helen at the movies? My mother wanted to know where I met you, and I told her Helen had introduced us. I couldn't think of anything else to say. I couldn't tell her we skipped school and went to the movies."

"Well, you should have warned me. I didn't know what to say," Then they both laughed.

As Philip stood in the late afternoon sun and waited for the streetcar, he thought about Doris and his feelings for her. These feelings were new to him. He had known a lot of girls as friends but had always been too busy with work and school for serious romantic involvements. He had wondered if, upon seeing her today, he would still feel the same way he had felt at their first meeting. He found that the attraction remained powerful and, if anything, was now even stronger. He wondered if she felt the same way about him. They hadn't been able to talk alone much today. He thought about her on the way back to camp and looked forward to their next meeting.

CHAPTER 5

Although it was late evening, it was not yet dark when Philip and Doris left the movie house. The setting sun reflecting on scattered clouds had turned the sky a deep red. It was going to be a beautiful evening. Salina Street was alive with bustling throngs of people going in and out of movie houses, theaters, and restaurants. Its voice rang out with the clanging of streetcar wheels meeting tracks, the squealing of brakes, the growls of bus and automobile engines, and the honking of horns. The late June air was warm and heavy with exhaust fumes that mingled with enticing aromas of cooking oils and spices drifting from the open doors of restaurants.

Philip had spent most of his life in a rural area. He liked the sights and sounds of the city, and he loved being there with Doris. They had seen a Mary Pickford film, and both had enjoyed it. He had stolen quick glances at Doris during the film and noticed that she had been totally absorbed. Now, as they walked up Salina Street, the sky was starting to darken, and street lights were turning on as marques were being lit up in theaters. Philip took Doris's hand and they looked at each other and smiled. They walked along in silence, not feeling the need for words, just happy being in each other's company.

Philip had received a letter from his mother that morning and in it were cautions about getting involved with a "city girl." Philip had tried to recall exactly what he had written about Doris and didn't think it had been much, but apparently, it had been enough for Nellie to discern his feelings. Her letter had contained worries about clever women out to trap unsuspecting young men and dire warnings to be careful lest he fall into one of these traps. Philip thought his mother overly imaginative and scoffed at the idea that Doris was trying to "trap" him. If anything, he was pursuing her! He also doubted that Doris had had any actual experience with men or that she had much knowledge of the feminine tricks or "traps" of which Nellie wrote. Philip decided he would make no further mention of Doris in his letters to his mother.

Doris's mother also had cautioned her about getting too "serious" with Philip but for different reasons. While she thought him a nice young man, he would soon be leaving Syracuse, perhaps never to return. He was very likely to meet someone else and forget all about her or, *although she didn't say this, be killed in the war.* In any case, she saw only heartbreak ahead for Doris and wished to shield her from it.

As Philip and Doris continued up the street toward their streetcar stop, they heard the shouts of a newsboy selling his papers. The headlines screamed out the latest news of the war in Europe, reminding the couple that Philip would soon be part of that war.

Doris asked, "Does hearing about the war make you afraid, knowing you will be there soon?"

Philip said, "No, not afraid, really. I mean, I know what could happen, but I knew that when I signed up. I'm hoping that I come out of it OK."

During the ride to Elmwood they both spoke of the events that were happening in their lives.

Doris said, "Helen is giving a Fourth of July party at her house. Would you like to go with me? Helen won't mind if I bring you."

Philip said, "Yes, I'd like to go. I'll try to get a pass for that day."

They got off the streetcar and walked up the hill to Doris's house. Once away from the bright lights of downtown, they were enveloped in a cloak of darkness as a riot of glittering stars shone above them. When they were outside Doris's house, Philip put his arms around her and tenderly kissed her. She responded eagerly, and they melted into each other's arms. At that moment, both knew they were in love. They clung to each other, wishing that moment would never end.

After a few minutes, they heard the sounds of footsteps coming from inside the house and Doris said, "I think my mother is coming."

They quickly parted just before Louise opened the door. Doris said goodnight to Philip and entered the house as Philip said, "I'll see you soon."

Doris felt breathless, and her heart was pounding. Her skin felt flushed and she hoped her mother didn't notice but, as she saw the way Louise was scrutinizing her, she knew she wasn't fooling her.

Louise said, "Did you like the film?"

Doris, trying to keep her voice steady, said, "Yes, Mary Pickford was the star. We both liked it."

Not wanting to answer any more of her mother's questions, Doris excused herself and quickly retired to her bedroom. She lay on her bed and thought about Philip, reliving every minute of the evening. She could still feel his touch and his kiss. She didn't know how she could live until she saw him again. She would count the days until July 4th.

On the ride back to camp, Philip's stomach was turning over, and his heart felt like it would burst from his chest. He didn't know if he could survive until he saw Doris again. He had found the love of his life, and all he wanted was to be with her.

CHAPTER 6

T he fourth of July started out with a thunderstorm, but by late
morning, the clouds had cleared, and the sun shone brightly,
drying everything out. The holiday party was an annual tradition
with the Shore family, but this year, with the USA now in the war
and the close proximity of Camp Syracuse, everyone was feeling
especially patriotic.

The Shores had set up a large tent in their yard, and Helen
and her brother and sister decorated it with red, white, and blue
streamers. These and the blooming rose bushes and early summer
flowers gave the yard a festive look. Helen and Doris had known
each other since childhood, having belonged to the same church,
but they became best friends when both entered Valley Academy
for high school. Many of their other friends from school were invited, as well as neighbors and friends of the Shores.

There was already a large group at the party by the time Philip
and Doris arrived that afternoon. Philip had duty that morning
and then had been given a pass for the rest of the day. There was
a festive mood among the partiers. Small groups were engaging
in conversation, lawn games were being played, and a few people
brought musical instruments and were taking turns playing them.

An assortment of food had been set out. There was ham, cold
fried chicken, sausages, salads, fruit, and cakes as well as tea and
lemonade. All this looked like a feast to Philip, accustomed as he

was to Army food. He found, however, that he didn't have much of an appetite while Doris was around and ate very little. Doris also only picked at her food. Both were experiencing the rather sick feelings of those newly in love, and eating was the furthest thing from their minds, being only interested in each other. They hoped to talk alone but didn't have much of a chance. Doris was popular among her friends, and they all wanted to greet her and were curious to meet her soldier friend. Finally, they had a chance to steal away.

They took a long walk in the surrounding neighborhood, holding each other's hands as they walked.

They stopped for a kiss, and Philip said, "I love you so much, Doris."

Her heart stopped, and she said breathlessly, "Oh, I love you, too, so much."

They kissed again and held each other in a long embrace, not knowing or caring about who might be watching from the windows of nearby houses. As they continued to walk, they talked about their future.

Doris said, "When do you think you will leave to go overseas?"

He said, "I don't have any idea. So far, no units have left the camp, but I suppose it could be any time. I'll see if I can find out, and then we can figure out what we should do."

When they returned to the party, no one seemed to have missed them, and they joined a group of Doris's friends. Later that night, Mr. Shore got out a large box of fireworks he had ordered and set off firecrackers and Roman candles on the front lawn. They had great fun watching them. It had been a wonderful day.

Philip asked his sergeant and then the lieutenant if they knew when the men were scheduled to leave to go overseas, but if either of them knew, they weren't telling him. When he talked to the other recruits, none of them seemed to have heard anything either. Philip supposed it could be anytime. They continued with training every day. He thought about going away and leaving Doris. She was so pretty and popular, she was sure to find someone else. In the past, he had never really given any thought to marriage. In fact, it had been the furthest thing from his mind, but he now debated with himself if he should ask her to marry him. He thought about it over the next several days, wondering what he should do.

When he saw her a few days later, they took a long walk in the park.

They found a secluded spot and, after a few passionate kisses, he made his decision, "I want to marry you."

Doris reacted with breathless excitement and surprise. She hadn't been expecting this but immediately said, "Yes, I want to marry you, too." She had the same fears that Philip had, that he would meet someone else once they were apart (she had heard stories about pretty French girls).

Philip thought they should waste no time and be married immediately. He said, "I'm going to speak to your father today."

They found Louise outside working in the garden. It was a warm day, and offering Philip a cold drink, the three entered the house where they found Horace sitting and reading the newspaper. After a few pleasantries, Philip wasted no time in asking Horace for permission to marry his daughter.

The Bowmans were somewhat taken aback but not entirely surprised. Louise, especially, had taken note of the lovesick expressions and adoring looks that passed between the couple when their eyes met and suspected they were in love *or at least what they think is love*, she thought. *They don't really know enough about each other or know what real love is.*

Horace said, "I think you're rushing into things. You don't know each other well enough to make a decision like that. You've only known each other for a short time." To Doris, he said, "Your mother and I like Philip and think he's a fine young man, but you are just too young, and I don't think you know what you are doing." He went on to say that it would be best to wait until Philip returned home from his overseas service. "Then, if you still feel the same, we will give you a nice wedding. I have some connections in the city, and I can help Philip get a good job."

Philip and Doris nodded but didn't say much and left the room without anything really being agreed on. However, the next time they were alone, they decided they didn't want to wait.

Doris said, " I'll be eighteen soon, and then I can do whatever I want. I won't need my father's permission."

Philip said, "Where should we get married?"

This presented a dilemma. Doris had always assumed that when the time came for her to be married, her wedding would be in the Elmwood Presbyterian Church, but now she said, "I can't ask my minister to marry us. He'll tell my parents."

Philip thought for a minute and said, " I'll try to figure something out. Maybe I'll ask Andy. He's from around here, and he may have an idea."

When Philip spoke to Andy, he told him that his church, The Liverpool Methodist Episcopal, had a kind minister who was understanding and enjoyed working with young people. He also had great feelings for the men in uniform. Andy promised to speak to him about marrying the couple. The next time Philip saw Doris, he told her Andy's minister had agreed to marry them as long as they were of age and had a marriage license. After inquiring around, he had been told that the license could be obtained at the courthouse. A plan was then put into place for the wedding to occur two days after Doris's eighteenth birthday. Philip would try to get time off a day or two before that so they could meet at the courthouse and purchase the license. Then, he hoped to get an overnight pass the following Saturday. If either of these plans fell through, they would need to postpone the wedding until a later time, but they hoped it would all work out. Due to their worries that Philip could be sent overseas at any time, they were afraid to wait too long. The Army might not allow the men any leaves once orders were issued, and it would then be too late.

Doris found her baptismal certificate in a family Bible, took it out, and hid it in her room, planning to use it as proof of her age.

They would need two witnesses for the marriage, and Andy Wise had already agreed to stand up with the couple. Doris also asked Helen Shore to accompany them. Although Helen was somewhat surprised at the suddenness of the marriage, she liked Philip and thought the whole idea of an elopement was exciting. She was thrilled to play a part in it and readily agreed.

CHAPTER 7

Doris spent her eighteenth birthday quietly. The Bowmans had never made a great fuss over birthdays, but Louise made a cake they enjoyed after a simple supper. The next afternoon, Philip and Doris met briefly at the courthouse and obtained their marriage license. Philip had been able to get permission to leave the camp for a short time by telling his superiors he needed to meet out-of-town visitors at the train station. His plan was to use these same visitors as his reason for requesting a weekend pass if they asked. He was worried that if they knew the real reason – that he was getting married, especially to a woman he had just recently met – they would try to talk him out of it. The men had already been warned about local women who had married soldiers to get allotment checks. He knew that wasn't the case with Doris, but didn't want to go through the ordeal of trying to convince them. Of course, they couldn't really stop him from marrying. After all, he had been old enough to join the Army, and he was old enough to get married, but they could delay things by denying him the pass and, instead, assigning him to some work detail for the weekend.

Doris awoke on Saturday morning to a beautiful day. The past few days had been extremely hot, but it had cooled off, and the humidity had lessened. Doris felt nervous and tried to keep herself busy, reading a book and helping Louise with some household chores, all the while watching the clock. Philip called her early that afternoon to tell her that there had been no problem with getting the weekend pass. Andy had also gotten a pass, so everything was to go off as scheduled. She then called Helen to finalize plans for meeting her.

The family ate an early supper, and then Doris headed for the streetcar stop where she was to meet Helen. She had packed a small bag, telling her mother that she and Helen had plans to attend a party given by one of their schoolmates, after which she would spend the night with Helen. She had done this at times in the past and Louise didn't think much about it. She was actually glad to see Doris spending less time with Philip and more time with her other friends. *Perhaps, with time, the relationship would cool.*

Philip and Andy left the camp a little earlier than they had planned. At the last minute, Philip remembered he would need a wedding ring for Doris. Andy had recommended a store where he could find one at a price that he could afford and, after stopping there on the way, got to the meeting place a little early. The two waited anxiously for the women to appear. As her streetcar approached the stop, Doris saw them both waiting for her, and her heart turned over. Philip smiled and waved as he watched Doris get off the streetcar. She was wearing a floral print dress and a small hat that was adorned with flowers, and he thought, *She looks so pretty! I'm the luckiest man in the world!* The couple greeted each other with a breathless kiss and the four headed off to catch another streetcar to Liverpool.

They got off the streetcar in front of the church and walked to the parsonage, which was right next door. The Reverend Benson had been waiting for them and greeted them with a smile. He examined their marriage license, and after a few questions, they proceeded with the marriage ceremony. The couple recited their vows, and Philip placed the ring he had purchased on Doris's finger. He had had to guess at the size and was grateful when it slipped on easily. Doris looked at the ring and smiled. Their hearts were overflowing with love for each other as they both said, "I do," and after Rev. Benson pronounced them man and wife, they shared their first kiss as a wedded couple. Neither had ever felt such happiness. Rev. Benson then shook hands with Philip and Andy, and Helen gave Doris a hug and a kiss. They then entered a small office where Rev. Benson filled out their marriage certificate.

The four young people left the parsonage, stepping out into the soft summer air. It was a lovely evening; the late-day sun was just starting to fade, and they all felt happy and in the mood for a celebration. Andy had taken his father into his confidence about the marriage, and Mr. Wise had given him a little money with instructions to treat the couple to a post-wedding supper. Andy suggested that they walk to the Cobblestone Inn. "It's not far from here," he said. "I've been there with my father. The manager is a friend of his."

The Cobblestone Inn was an old saloon that had been built by one of the salt industry barons and was a favorite among locals. It featured a small dining area where they entered, walking across the sawdust-covered floor and making their way to a corner table. The usual saloon smells were present – spilled beer, fried food, and unwashed bodies. The room was quiet, but the few patrons who were present looked up and smiled at the men in their uniforms. Andy signaled the barman, and when he approached their table, he asked, "Is Mr. Carson in tonight?"

"Yes," he said. "I think he's in the kitchen. Would you like to speak to him?"

"Yes, tell him it's Jack Wise's son, Andy."

After a short time, the barman returned with a middle-aged man. "Andy!" he said. "I'm surprised to see you! Your father told me you'd joined the Army. You've brought some friends with you."

Andy introduced his three friends and then said, "Philip and Doris just got married."

Philip stood, and Mr. Carson shook his hand and smiled at the two women. Looking at Philip, he said, "Congratulations to you and your pretty bride."

Turning to Andy, he then said," I've known this young man since he was just a little boy. Now he's getting ready to go off to war!" He turned to the barman and said, "Bring these young people whatever they want to eat and drink. It's on the house."

The four thanked him profusely, and after he left, Andy and Philip each ordered a glass of beer. Doris and Helen looked at each other. Although both had been to tea rooms and soda shoppes, neither had ever eaten in a saloon and were unsure what to order. The barman suggested the women might each like a glass of wine, and Doris and Helen both nodded in agreement. They all then ordered the house special of sausages and potatoes with fresh vegetables. Philip and Doris found they were too excited to eat much, but the four laughed and talked, taking great pleasure in each other's company. Doris took small sips of her wine, finding its somewhat sharp flavor unfamiliar to her palate but, nonetheless, enjoying it. Philip couldn't take his eyes from her, thinking how lovely she looked in the soft glow of the waning sun as it shone through the window.

Halfway through the meal, Andy left the table and crossed the room, where he was seen talking with Mr. Carson. The two men returned to the table, and Mr. Carson looked at Philip and Doris and said, "I have a room on the second floor that hasn't been rented for tonight, and I would be happy to have you stay there at no charge."

The couple looked at each other and at Mr. Carson, nodding gratefully. Doris felt a shiver of excitement as she thought of spending the night in a room alone with Philip, who felt great relief, not having been sure where they would spend their wedding night. He had originally thought about going downtown and finding a hotel but had to spend some of his money on the ring for Doris, leaving him a little short. He was now filled with gratitude toward Andy and Mr. Carson.

The evening continued to pass pleasantly until finally, Andy rose from the table and said he would see Helen home and then return to the camp. The two said their goodbyes and Philip and Doris were left alone at the table. The saloon was now starting to fill up and had become noisier, and they decided to withdraw to the privacy of their room. They were given a key, and glowing with happiness, they ascended the stairs to the second floor. Their room was one of the older ones and somewhat shabby, with worn carpet, faded wallpaper, and cooking odors that drifted up from the ground-floor kitchen. As the saloon crowd became more boisterous, the sounds of their talk and laughter penetrated the walls of their room. Philip and Doris were aware of none of this, absorbed as they were in their love for each other. They spent the night in each other's arms, talking at times about the distant future after the war was over and their hopes for a home and family. They tried not to think about the immediate future – that Philip would soon be leaving for the war and how their little world was about to be torn apart, much as the greater world was being torn apart by the war raging in Europe. For now, they had this night and each other.

As they lay in bed together, Doris said, "Oh, Philip, I 'm so happy!" I wish this night could last forever."

"I know," Philip said, "I don't want it to end either."

They tried to hold on to the night by staying awake, but eventually, sleep overtook them both. When they awoke, the first rays of the sun were coming through the window in their room, replacing the glow of the street lamp. Late that morning, they left the inn and caught the streetcar back to the city and then transferred to one to Elmwood. Doris said, "When do you have to be back to the camp?"

Philip said, "Not until later this afternoon. I want to be with you when you tell your parents."

She said, "I wonder if my father will be home. He may be working today." Horace was a railroad engineer and his schedule was somewhat irregular, sometimes having to work on Sunday.

It was early afternoon by the time they arrived at the Bowman house. Both parents were at home, and the air in the house was filled with the aroma of roasting meat. Horace and Louise looked up in surprise when the young couple entered. Louise said, "Why, Philip, I didn't expect to see you today." To Doris, she said, "Did you go to church with the Shores? We didn't go this morning. Your father got home very late last night and felt too tired to go."

Wasting no time, Doris blurted out, "We got married last night."

Louise said, "Married? What do you mean?"

"We got married by a minister in Liverpool," Doris said.

Louise looked from one to the other and then at Horace, who said. "You went off and got married after we had all agreed you would wait."

Philip then said, "We didn't want to wait, sir. We wanted to be married before I left for the war."

Louise then sat down and started to cry. Horace stared at them and looked as if he were at a loss for words. Normally a reserved, rather stoic man, he now appeared to be in a state of shock. "How could you do this? You promised you would wait."

"Well, we didn't really promise," Doris said.

Horace glared at her. "You know what I meant, young lady. It was understood you were going to wait." To Philip, he said, "And to think I trusted you with my daughter." To Doris, he said, "We never expected anything like this from you." These words were barely out of his mouth when he realized that just the opposite was true and thought, *This is exactly what we should have expected from Doris.*

Horace threw up his hands and then began pacing a small area in the room, deep in thought. Louise continued to cry softly while Philip and Doris stood helplessly watching. Horace finally pointed to the couple and said, "Sit down."

Horace was thinking, *Maybe this is for the best after all. Perhaps it's better that they are married.* He had seen the way the two looked at each other and how they could hardly keep their hands off each other. He recognized passion when he saw it, and Doris had always been a strong-willed girl. *Who knew what might have happened if things had continued as they were? They might even have conceived a child out of wedlock! That would have killed Louise.* He looked at his wife and thought, *Well, we both had our dreams for Doris, but those dreams will now need to be put aside. What's done is done. No, it was probably best that Doris was now safely married.*

The four continued to sit in silence. Finally, Horace said, "Dry your tears, Mother. What's done is done, and nothing can change things now." He pulled his handkerchief from his pocket and handed it to his wife, who sniffled softly and blew her nose. To Philip and Doris, he said, "Well, you've made your bed, and now you will have to lie in it. If you've made a mistake, you're the ones who will have to live with it, but we'll do what we can to help you."

Doris said, "Thank you, Dad."

"Thank you, sir," said Philip, "I promise to be a good husband to Doris."

A thought suddenly occurred to Horace. "Does your mother know about this?" he asked Philip.

"No sir, I haven't told her yet. I plan to do that today."

"Well, I think you should do it right now. You can use our telephone." He pointed toward the hallway.

"Um, they don't have a telephone," Philip said. Although telephones were now commonplace in many homes, the Osborns still didn't have one, as the service had not yet reached all the rural areas.

"No telephone?"

"No sir, I plan to write to her today."

Horace sighed, and they sat for a few more minutes. Next, there was a flurry of awkward kisses, and Horace shook his new son-in-law's hand.

After a time, Louise looked at the clock and said, "Well, I suppose we should think about eating. Dinner should be ready soon. Doris, come and help me in the kitchen." The women then rose and left the room, leaving the two men alone to engage in awkward conversation.

Louise had cooked a pot roast and vegetables for their Sunday dinner, and Doris helped her with the final preparations before they sat down to eat. Philip and Doris, now safely married and having gotten through the ordeal of breaking the news to the Bowmans, suddenly realized they hadn't eaten in several hours and were hungry. They felt happy and content and ate heartily. Horace and Louise barely touched their food.

After they finished eating, Philip said he should be getting back to camp. Doris walked with him to the door, and they held each other tightly and kissed goodbye.

Doris said, "I can't believe we are really married."

Philip smiled and said, "I'll see you as soon as I can," and left.

After he left, Doris helped her mother clear the table and wash and dry the dishes. They worked mostly in silence, everything seeming to already have been said. After they finished, she excused herself and went into her bedroom and lay on her bed. She thought about Philip, missing him already. She thought about how it would be when he left to go off to war, and she didn't want him to go. Tears welled up in her eyes and, though she tried to stop them, spilled over and ran down her cheeks. She didn't know what to do next. She realized she hadn't slept much the previous night, and her tiredness was making it hard to think. She closed her eyes, intending to take a short nap, but when she awoke, the room was dark. She got up and prepared for bed and then slept the remainder of the night.

When Philip got back to camp, Andy was in their tent, along with some of their other friends. Andy had already told them the news about Philip's marriage, and there were handshakes and hearty congratulations, as well as several jokes. One of the men spoke jokingly about him now having a ball and chain.

Philip just smiled, and Andy said, "A very pretty ball and chain," and they all laughed.

Some of the men in their group of friends had met girls in Syracuse, and some had even gotten engaged, but Philip was the first among them to marry. Now he said, " I guess I should go find Sarge and tell him."

When he saw the sergeant and told him he had gotten married, Philip thought he didn't look happy about it, but the sergeant only said, "Go tell them in the office so they can change your records."

On the way back to his tent, he thought about the fact that he was now married but would soon be leaving his new wife. He had been so excited about going to war but was now having misgivings. It didn't look as appealing as it once had. If anything happened to him, Doris would be a widow. The thought then struck him that they might conceive a child, and then he thought, *For all I know, we may have already done that last night! If I'm killed in the war, I could be leaving not only a widow but a fatherless child – one I will never know, and Doris will be left to raise alone!* He thought of his own mother and her struggles as a widow raising two sons, finally being forced into what, in his mind, had been a loveless marriage.

Thinking of his mother reminded him that he still hadn't told her of his marriage. As the Osborns didn't have a telephone, he'd have to tell her the news by letter, but not today. He'd write to her tomorrow. He'd write to Charlie, too, and his grandparents. As he sat down heavily on his bed, he suddenly felt overwhelmed and overcome with exhaustion. He lay back, closed his eyes, and fell into a dreamless sleep, which lasted until he was awakened for the first call the following morning.

CHAPTER 8

The rest of the summer moved along like a river flowing to the sea, with Philip and Doris adrift on its current. The two spent their days hoping and waiting for those times they could be together and then clinging for dear life to those moments once they arrived, all the while knowing there would be no escape from the ocean of unhappiness that awaited them. Each day brought them closer to the time when Philip would be sent off to war.

Camp Syracuse was now fully open, and the flow of new men had slowed to a trickle. The tents had all been set up, and most of the time was spent in training. When the men weren't doing that, they were given other tasks such as "policing" the grounds – picking up litter and cigarette butts. It seemed to Philip that the purpose of many of these activities was to keep the men busy as they waited for their overseas orders. He had little to complain of, however, as he was often able to get a pass to leave the camp when he asked for one.

Whenever he managed to get away, he would head for Elmwood to spend the time with Doris. Now that he was a married man, he was often allowed an overnight pass, and he would stay the night in Doris's bedroom. The fact that the Bowmans and Philip didn't know each other well, along with the suddenness of the marriage, made the situation somewhat awkward, but after a time, everyone settled in and made the best of it. Times when the four of them were together, such as meals, became more relaxed as they all got used to each other. Doris's grandmother, Jennie Bogardus, sometimes joined them for dinner. Jennie was a widow whose second husband had met with an unfortunate accident and drowned in Onondaga Creek several years before. In spite of this, Jennie had a cheerful personality that lightened the mood at the table, and Philip liked her very much. She had given the couple a china bowl that had been in her family as a wedding present, and Doris treasured it.

The summer weather was pleasant, and the couple often took advantage of it to get out of the house, if only for a walk in the park. On one of the last days in August, Doris packed a picnic lunch and headed downtown to Clinton Square. From there, she took a trolley along the west shore of Onondaga Lake. When the trolley got to the Pleasant Beach stop, which was near Camp Syracuse, Philip was waiting. Doris waved to him from the window, and he got on there. They continued to Long Branch Amusement Park at the northern end of the Lake.

Once in the park, they sat on the grass and ate the meat sandwiches and cookies Doris had brought. The park was filled with families making the most of the warm weather. The screams and shouts of children enjoying the rides could be heard throughout the park. Doris had been coming to the park since she was a child and loved the rides. Philip had attended the Calhoun County Fair back home in Michigan many times and always looked forward to the rides there as well. The ones in Long Branch Park were bigger and more permanent, and he was eager to try them.

The rides cost ten cents each, and the couple spent several minutes engaging in conversation about which ones they would spend their limited funds on. They immediately agreed on the merry-go-round and rode that.

Then Doris said, "I want to go on the roller coaster."

Philip said, "Okay, but only if we can go on the aerial swings after that."

Having come to an agreement, they headed for the roller coaster. Philip held on to Doris, who screamed throughout the ride. When it was over, they were both laughing and breathless with excitement. They then went on the aerial swings, which they both enjoyed but agreed did not compare to the thrill of the roller coaster, so they decided to splurge on one more ride on it.

They walked along the midway, where Philip won a small teddy bear for Doris by knocking over some dolls on a shelf. The midway had a small booth where an artist sat, offering to draw portraits for a price. He had no customers at the time, so Philip approached him about doing a small pencil sketch of Doris. Philip had asked Doris for a photograph of herself, and she had given him one from a family collection, but he liked the idea of the drawing. A price was negotiated, and Doris sat while the artist drew the picture.

When he finished, the couple remarked on what a good likeness it was; Philip said, "Looks just like you."

"It does," Doris said.

Philip paid the man, folded the drawing, and put it in his pocket. Doris smiled up at him and nestled closer to him.

They walked leisurely through the grounds of the park. Philip had been given an overnight pass, and they were in no hurry to leave and return to the more confining atmosphere of the Bowman household. The Bowmans were kind, but Philip continued to feel like a guest when he was there. He and Doris felt freer to be themselves when they were off on their own. They sat by the lake and looked out at the sun reflected on the water. A few of the leaves on the surrounding trees had already started to change color, reminding them that summer was coming to an end. Philip had heard that Camp Syracuse was scheduled to close down for the winter and reopen in the spring. The soldiers were housed in tents that were not heated or winterized in any way and, therefore, would be unable to withstand the assault of a Central New York winter. Due to this, he knew for sure he would be leaving sometime that autumn.

They sat inconsequentially conversing until Doris said, "Do you ever wish that you didn't have to leave – not go to war?"

Philip said, "Yes, I've thought that at times, but I know it's important, and someone has to do it." Then he said, "There have been times when I've wished I never signed up, but then I remember that if I hadn't, I wouldn't have come here, and we'd never have met. I hate to think about that." Doris moved closer to him as if the nearness of her body could somehow shield him from what was to come.

They stayed in the park until late afternoon, caught the trolley back to Clinton Square, and made their way to Elmwood for the night. During the ride, Philip took the small drawing of Doris from his pocket and unfolded it.

He said, "I'll take this with me wherever I go. Whenever I look at it, I'll remember today." Doris took his hand and rested her head on his shoulder, wishing the day could somehow go on forever.

CHAPTER 9

Earlier that week, Philip had finally heard from his mother. He had written to her, as well as his brother, Charlie, and his grandparents, right after he had married Doris and, although Charlie had immediately written back expressing his happiness and saying he couldn't wait to meet his new sister, he had also said, "I don't think Mother is happy about it."

He had also heard from his grandparents, who had been surprised by his news but sent their good wishes. From his mother, there had been only silence until almost a month passed. When her letter did come, it was short and somewhat stilted. She wrote:

Dear Philip,

I was surprised by your news, but I suppose I shouldn't have been. You have always seemed to know what you wanted to do and have rarely paid heed to what I thought was best for you. I only hope you have not made a serious mistake, but what is done is done, and I wish you the best. I will look forward to the time when I can meet the young woman.

With regards,
Your loving mother

Philip had written back, saying, "I can't wait for you to meet Doris. I know you will love her as I do, and she will love you." He wasn't entirely sure of this, but he hoped she would eventually come to accept Doris and be happy for him. Philip loved his mother but thought her old fashioned with outdated ideas, especially about women. He didn't want his love for his wife to cause a barrier between them. He also thought his mother was likely influenced by his stepfather. In any case, there wasn't much he could do about it at present. He had other things on his mind as he prepared to go to war, and the situation within his family would just have to work itself out.

In view of all this, Philip was greatly surprised when a few days later, he received another letter from his mother.

Dear Philip,

I have decided to make a trip to visit you. I want to see you before you leave to go to war and so does Charlie. I have been thinking about it for a while and have been setting aside a little of my household money each week. I still didn't have enough, so I spoke to your Grandfather Smith and he said he would give me the rest of the money to pay for the train fare for Charlie and me. Do you know of a place where we could stay that wouldn't cost too much? We won't be able to stay long as your stepfather needs us on the farm. We want to come soon, but I will wait to hear from you before I purchase our tickets.

With regards,
Your loving mother

Dear Mother,

I'm glad you and Charlie are going to come. If you can, try to be here on a Sunday as that is visitor's day at the camp and you will be able to visit and I can show you around. I talked to the

Bowmans and Doris's grandmother, Jennie Bogardus, said you and Charlie can stay with her. She lives nearby and has an extra room you can stay in. If you let me know what time your train will be in, my father-in-law, Horace Bowman, can meet your train and drive you in his motorcar. I'll be glad to see you and have you meet Doris.

Your loving son,
Philip

Nellie and Charlie made the train trip to Syracuse soon after that, staying for two days. They visited the camp on Sunday and met some of Philip's friends, including Andy Wise. Philip showed them the tent where he slept, the mess hall, and the new YMCA that was being built. Charlie, especially, was interested in seeing the grounds where his brother trained, including a practice trench. Jennie Bogardus provided them with a comfortable room and Louise Bowman invited them to supper one of the evenings. Charlie had brought his violin, and in the evening, he entertained them with his repertoire of songs, some of which they sang along with. Doris also played some songs on the piano. Nellie wasn't quite sure about Doris. She was nice enough but seemed a bit flashy with her bright red lipstick and skirts that were a little shorter than Nellie thought was proper. She did seem to be from a good family, though, and she was grateful for that.

Before they left, Nellie gave Philip a scarf she had knitted for him, saying, "This will keep you warm on cold winter nights." She had tears in her eyes as she said goodbye, not knowing if she would ever see her son again. Philip also felt sad as he gave his mother a kiss on the cheek and shook hands with Charlie.

Summer soon became autumn, and the air turned cooler. The

ground was now often covered with frost in the morning, and the trees were changing from lush green to vivid shades of yellow, orange, and red. The days were shortening, and Philip became increasingly aware that his time in the recruit camp would soon be coming to an end.

Philip and Andy had been in Company H of the 16th Infantry since arriving at Camp Syracuse, but early in August, Andy was transferred to another unit. They had hoped to stay together for the remainder of their time at the recruit camp and then go to France together, but it wasn't to be.

Philip had said, "I hate to see you go."

"You know where I am; we'll still see each other," Andy had said. They did see each other when they both had free time and sometimes during meals at the mess hall, but both had been aware that this change brought them another step closer to the war.

One day in October, Andy told Philip that his mother wanted to invite him and Doris to Sunday dinner if they could both get passes.

Philip said, "Sure, I'll ask Doris."

When he asked her, she said, "Yes, I'd like to meet the Wises."

The three took the Liverpool trolley and walked from the stop to Andy's parents' house. The Wises congratulated Philip and Doris on their marriage. Mrs. Wise then surprised Doris with a silver spoon that was engraved with a "B" for Boughton. Doris was pleased and touched. A few of the people from their church, including the Shores, had sent the couple small gifts upon hearing of the marriage, and Jennie Bogardus had given them the bowl, but they had received few wedding gifts.

Doris was close to tears as she said, "Oh, thank you so much. I'll put this away to use when we have our own home after the war is over."

The dinner conversation soon turned to the war, Andy saying, "Another unit left Pleasant Beach this week to go to France."

Philip said, "I heard a big crowd of people came out, as usual, to see them off."

Then Doris said, "Yes, one of my friends was there, and she said people were waving flags and cheering for the men."

Mrs. Wise said, "I'm so proud of Andy for signing up, but I can't help worrying about him."

"Oh, I'll be alright, Mom," Andy said.

Philip said, "I think once we get there, we will quickly win the war – the Germans won't know what hit them." These words fell easily from his lips as he had heard them often from other recruits and from some of the officers.

Mr. Wise said, "I'm not sure the Germans will be so easy to defeat. A lot of English boys have been killed, French, too." Many people, Andy's father among them, had read the newspaper accounts of the terrible losses incurred by the British and French in the war.

Philip and Andy looked at each other. They also knew of the perils they would face on the war front. They had had this conversation between themselves when they were alone. They had heard about the trenches and no man's land. In addition to this, one of their officers, who had seen action in the Spanish-American War, had given an honest accounting of what it was like to be on a battlefield. However, neither said anything, and silence prevailed until Mrs. Wise changed the subject by remarking on the nice weather they were having and the beauty of the fall leaves.

At the end of the afternoon, Philip and Doris left to go back to Elmwood, while Andy planned to spend the night at his parents' home. Both men had been given an overnight pass and didn't have to return to the camp until the following morning.

During the ride home, Doris said, "The Wises are really nice."

Philip said, "Yeah, I like them a lot."

Doris then said, "They're really worried about Andy."

"I still think he'll be okay," Philip said. In truth, he wasn't at all sure, but didn't want Doris to know that. He knew what she was really thinking. She was just as worried about him. Instinctively, he reached over and took her hand.

Doris made no reply and the rest of the trip was made in silence.

Later that month, both Philip and Andy received their orders. Andy was to ship off for France in early November, and Philip two weeks later. On Andy's final day at camp, Philip went to his tent and sat on his bed, talking to him as he packed and prepared to leave.

Andy said, "Tell Doris I said goodbye."

"I will," Philip said. "Hey, maybe you'll meet a nice French girl."

Andy laughed and said, "Yeah, that would be great."

Then Philip said, "Well, take care of yourself. Maybe we'll run into each other over there."

"Maybe, but if not, we'll see each other when we get back. You're coming back here to Syracuse, aren't you?"

"Sure, my wife is here, and my father-in-law promised to help me find a good job."

As Andy left and they shook hands a final time, both hoped this wasn't the end of their friendship and there would be many more good times after the war.

Philip felt a sense of loneliness every time he walked past Andy's empty tent. The whole camp now seemed forlorn and empty as Philip's unit would be one of the last to leave before it closed down for the winter. He now just wanted to leave and begin the next phase of his life – the war. The sooner he went, the sooner he would be back and he and Doris could begin their life together.

The next several days were filled with stepped-up training and instruction. The men were issued mess kits and other equipment and their records were checked off to make sure they had received all their inoculations. Philip was promoted to Private First Class. Passes were harder to get now, but Philip managed to get an overnight pass so he could spend one last night with Doris.

They had a quiet dinner and, after spending a short time talking to the Bowmans, the couple retired to the privacy of Doris's room. After a prolonged embrace, Philip said, "Well, I guess this will be it. My unit will be leaving soon. I'll call you when I know exactly when."

Doris then said, "I have something to tell you. I'm going to have a baby," she blurted out. She went on, "I've thought so for a while, but now I'm sure. My mother thinks it will be born in June."

Philip just stared, his mouth open. He was stunned by the news, although he wasn't sure why. He'd always known it was a possibility but had hoped it wouldn't happen – not until he was back from the war.

Doris also wasn't really happy about having a baby while Philip was away but wanted to put up a brave front and had hoped for the best – that Philip would be happy about it. With slumped shoulders and a sad expression, she said, "You're not happy about it."

He immediately caught himself and said, "Oh no, I am happy. I just wasn't expecting it, and I'm worried about you being alone when the baby is born." Then he put his arms around her, pulled her close, and said, "I hope the baby is a girl who looks just like you."

Doris said, "Maybe the war will be over quickly, and you'll be back before it's born.

Philip forced a smile and said, "Well, yeah, maybe. We can hope for that."

That night, Philip had a difficult time falling asleep, and once he did, he was restless, tossing and turning most of the night. He awoke in the middle of the night to discover the full moon shining brightly through the window, lighting up the room. He looked at Doris and saw that she was also awake, her eyes wide open. He reached over and pulled her to him.

She started to cry softly and said, "I don't want you to go."

He only said, "I know."

The two slept little the remainder of the night and had little appetite for breakfast the next morning. When they said their final goodbye at the door, Philip said. "I'll call you when I know what time we're leaving."

Doris said, "I want to go to the station to see you off."

After a final kiss, Philip headed down the hill toward South Avenue and the streetcar stop. When he reached the intersection, he turned and waved. Doris watched him until he was out of sight.

Philip called Doris the next day to tell her he would be leaving from the Pleasant Beach station at 10:30 the following day.

Doris said, "I'll be there. My father is going to drive me. I'll be wearing my red hat."

He said, "I'll look for you. I love you."

The next day, when he marched to the train station with his company, he looked over at the small group of citizens waiting on the platform, and there was Doris, standing with her father and waving to him. Their eyes met briefly as he watched her blow him a kiss and that was the last he saw of her.

Now, he sat in his seat on the train as it moved south along the tracks. The men from his unit sat all around him, some talking excitedly and others more subdued. Philip thought of all that had happened since that fateful day when he had, on impulse, gone to the recruiting office in Battle Creek, Michigan, and enlisted in the Army. He had changed so much from the hopeful student who had only wanted to leave the farm and become a war hero. He was now a husband who would soon become a father and was on his way to join a war in which many would die. Well, he would do his best to be a good soldier, and he was willing to die for his country if that was what was required of him, but he would also try his hardest to get through the war in one piece and return to Doris and their child.

PART II
WAR

CHAPTER 10

December 10, 1917

Dear Doris,
We made it across the ocean, and I am now in France. I'm not allowed to tell you where I am, but I'm here waiting to be sent to another zone, where we will receive more training.

We crossed on a British ship, and the trip took two weeks. We went with a group of about 20 ships, and the American navy protected us. The sea was rough sometimes, and I got sick because the ship rocked back and forth a lot. Many of us had never been to sea before or had even seen the ocean, and we felt afraid at times that the ship would capsize. Also, the ships had to watch for German submarines that might try to sink them.

I can't tell you how good it is to once again be on dry land! It's cold here, but today is a sunny day. The French people are very nice and seem to like the American soldiers. Some of them speak English, some just a few words, and some quite a lot. There is a canteen here where I was able to buy writing paper and stamps, and I also bought a little book with common French words that I use so I can at least say hello and things like thank you.

There is a mess kitchen here, and the food is not too bad – typical Army food, but better than on the ship. I have worked in the kitchen a couple of times doing KP. Right now, they have given us some free time so we could write letters home, but usually we are working. They always find something for us to do. That's the Army!

You can write to me at the above address. Be sure to include my number 43391. They said as long as you do that, they will find me no matter where I am, and I will get your letters. I love you and miss you very much. Here's hoping the war will end soon and we will be together again.

Your loving husband,
Philip

December 12, 1917

Dear Mother,
I finally arrived in France and am here waiting to be sent to another zone where I will train with French and British officers. The trip across the ocean was fine but the ship was crowded and I got sick a couple of times when we hit rough seas. I'm fine now. It was raining when we got here, but today is sunny and cold.

The French people we have met on the streets have smiled and been very nice. They seem to be glad we are here. They have lived with this war for a long time, and I think they're hoping that now that we are here, it will finally end. We've met a few French children and have been able to practice our French words with them.

I didn't have time to write to you before I left, but Doris promised to write to you, and I hope that she did. I'm sending my address so you can write to me and give me news from home. Please remember me to Grandmother and Grandpa and tell Charlie I will write to him soon.

Your son,
Philip

Philip had set sail from Hoboken, New Jersey, on November 22 on the British ship Carpathia. The ship had been crowded, and the trip was extremely uncomfortable. He, as well as many others, had become ill when the ship hit rough seas. The odor of vomit, along with other bodily discharges, permeated the enclosed lower decks where the men spent most of their time, adding to the unpleasant conditions. They were allowed to go up on deck once or twice a day for fresh air and exercise and to participate in life-boat drills but were otherwise confined below.

The men soon grew tired of the food. Breakfast consisted of bacon, bread and jam, and porridge. Stew with turnips, carrots, and potatoes was served for the late afternoon meal, which the British called "Tea."

The voyage had taken them to Liverpool, England, and after a short stop there, proceeded down the coast and across the channel, landing at St. Nazaire, France. Philip stayed there for several days before being marched to a railway station where he, along with others from his 16th Infantry Unit, boarded a train to Gondrecourt in the eastern part of France. There, the men received their first real training from French officers. They joined other companies of the 16th Infantry, which, along with several other brigades, would comprise the First Expeditionary Division, under the direct command of General John "Black Jack" Pershing, and eventually became known as the Big Red One.

At Gondrecourt, the troops were taught the basics of trench warfare using a network of practice trenches that had been constructed on the grounds. The men were taught to handle and use trench warfare weapons as they learned to live and fight in the trenches.

The weather that year was brutally cold and was said to be the worst anyone in France could remember. The men spent long days outside in the cold, conditioning, drilling, and marching with their heavy packs, which contained everything they owned. Periodically, the men would be rotated out to an area between Nancy and Luneville, where they conducted exercises in open warfare, which included bayonet training and target practice using rifles. They learned about machine guns, artillery, and ground tactics. The cold weather, mud, ice, and snow made the training extremely difficult. Philip had experienced cold, snowy winters growing up on the farm in Michigan, but many of the men were from southern states and were not accustomed to this kind of weather. After a few weeks of this open warfare training, the men would return to Gondrecourt and continue the trench warfare training.

CHAPTER 11

Philip's mail caught up with him at Gondrecourt, and he received a packet of letters and a package.

Doris wrote:
January 10, 1918

Dear Philip,
I have received two letters from you and am glad you had a safe voyage. We had a quiet Christmas, celebrating with a small dinner with my Grandmother Jennie and Uncle Eugene.

It's been cold here, and we had a snowstorm last week. Now, the snow is melting a little. Mother and I have been meeting with a group of ladies at the church and knitting socks for the soldiers. We learned a new British method of knitting socks without seams. I haven't finished mine yet, but one of the ladies gave me a pair she made to send to you.

I sent them in a package along with a tin of cookies made from an old recipe from my father's family. The man in the post office assured me that packages are being sent to the troops every day, and they are being handled with care.

I want to tell you that I did write to your mother as you asked. I told her that you got off on November 20, as scheduled, and I also told her about the baby. I received a letter from her in return, thanking me for the news and telling me she was happy to hear that we are expecting a baby.

I am well, and our baby is growing. I miss you and love you very much. It's lonely here without you. Please stay safe and try hard to stay out of harm's way. I think so often of the day you will return to me.

Your loving wife,
Doris

Philip smiled as he read the letter. *I can just imagine Doris sitting in a circle with a group of ladies and knitting. It must be hard for her. She likes to go to parties and have fun. But she is trying her best to be a good wife.* He wrote back:

February 1, 1918

Dear Doris,
I have received two letters from you, as well as the package you sent. The cookies were very good. Some were broken but still tasted good. I shared them with some of my friends here and all enjoyed them. I'm wearing the socks you sent right now and they are very warm. We need warm clothes here as it has been very cold and we spend the whole day outside. We spend the night in the buildings of deserted homes and farms.

I can't tell you where I am except to say that the country has been terribly torn up by the war. I feel sorry for the French people who have been living with this war for so long. Many of them have lost nearly everything, but still, they are friendly and kind to us.

I will go now and get back to work. We were given some time off to write letters. I'll write again soon. I love you very, very much and you are always in my thoughts and in my dreams.

With love from your husband,
Philip

Philip greatly missed Andy Wise and wondered where he was. He hadn't heard anything about Andy since he had left Camp Syracuse but hadn't really expected to. *Well, I know where Andy's parents live, he thought, and if I don't run into him over here, we'll see each other when the war is over – if only we both make it back alive.*

Several of the men in his unit had been with him at Camp Syracuse, but he had made new friends as well. One of them, Joe Kowalski, was a Polish boy from Toledo, Ohio. Philip and Joe were often assigned to duty together and had become good friends.

Sometimes in the evening, the two men would take shelter in a corner of an old stone barn, talking and smoking. Sometimes, on clear nights, they could hear the sounds of gunfire coming from the distant front lines. They often talked of home and family. Philip talked of his marriage to Doris, and Joe had admired the picture he had shown him. Joe's father owned a small store in Toledo, where Joe had worked before he enlisted and to which he planned to return after the war. "Someday, the store will be mine," he said.

Joe showed Philip a picture of a pretty blonde girl, saying, "This is my girlfriend, Anne."

Philip looked at the picture and said, "Wow, are you gonna marry her?"

Joe said, "I don't know. I want to, but her parents don't want her to marry me. They don't think I'm good enough for their only daughter."

"Not good enough?"

"Anne is from one of the old Toledo families, and her father is a big shot at one of the banks in town. They don't like the idea of their daughter marrying a Polish Catholic kid whose father owns a little store."

Philip said, "Well, I think you should marry her."

Joe said, "Maybe. It's complicated. Anne doesn't want to go against her parents. My worry is that she will meet someone else while I'm gone."

Philip said, "I know. I had the same worries. That's why Doris and I just went off on our own and got married."

Joe said, "That would cause a whole new set of problems. My parents would want me to be married in the church, and Anne isn't Catholic, so as I said, it's complicated."

Philip only nodded. This was an area in which he had little knowledge, but when he thought about Doris, he realized how lucky he was. *I have the most wonderful girl in the world waiting for me at home, and she's all mine.*

February 5, 1918

Dear Charlie,

I hope things are going well on the farm. I miss all of you very much. We are in a very war-torn part of France. I can't tell you where, but right now, this area is quiet as the action has moved elsewhere. We spend long days out in the cold, learning to fight in trenches and on open ground.

I still haven't seen any real action, but I suspect that day is coming. We are trained by French officers who also train our own officers in the French fighting methods.

I have made a lot of good friends here, but I miss my buddy, Andy Wise, from Camp Syracuse. There are several dogs that hang around the camp. I guess they have become separated from their French families and are surviving as best they can. There is one who hangs around our unit most of the time that the men have named Spike. We feed him scraps of food, and he rewards us by crawling in beside one of us on cold nights and keeping us warm. I'm reminded of the dogs we had on the farm. Mother would let them into the house on cold winter nights, and they always seemed to find their way into your bed!

Please write again when you have time.

Your brother,
Phil

CHAPTER 12

February 15, 1918

Dear Philip,
I have been getting your letters, sometimes more than one at a time. I'm glad you're safe and glad you liked the cookies and socks I sent. I still meet with the ladies of the church every week to knit socks for the soldiers.

Also, we are now eating less meat, sugar, and butter so that more will be available to be sent to our troops. People are being told to use less gasoline, so my father now takes the streetcar to work instead of driving his motorcar. We are supposed to have gasless Sundays, but we did drive to church last Sunday. Because of my condition, my father didn't want me to walk in the cold.

The photographer sent me the photographs we had taken before you left and I'm sending you one with this letter. My parents both said they thought it was a very good likeness of both of us, and they framed the larger one and placed it on the mantel. I sent one to your mother as well.

I went to see the midwife who will deliver our baby. She examined me and told me everything is progressing normally and I'm in good health. She said, as my mother thought, that she expected the baby to be born in June.

I love you and miss you very much and send many kisses with this letter.

Your loving wife,
Doris

February 15, 1918

Dear Philip,
Charlie and I have both received your letters. It's cold here, too, but the farm work must go on. Your stepfather has been ailing with a heavy cold, so Charlie and I have had to do more work, but there is nothing to be done about it.

When I have time, I'm trying to do some knitting for our men at the front. Several of the ladies at our church are doing that. We are all trying to do what we can for the war effort. Several others have boys who are fighting as well. Prayers are said every week in church for our men.

I have received two letters from Doris. She has told me about the baby, and I will try to knit some booties or something as well. Please try to stay safe and out of harm's way. Your grandparents send their love, and we all think of you every day.

With love,
Mother

March 1, 1918

Dear Doris,
I got your letter and the photograph you sent. I remember the day we met downtown to have the picture taken. I hadn't really wanted to do it, but am now glad that your parents insisted on it, and agree that it's a very good likeness. I put the picture in my pack along with other ones I have of you. I still have the drawing that was made the

day we met at Long Branch Park and take it out often and always smile when I look at it. I remember that day so well and the fun we had. Here's hoping we will have many more good times like that when I am home from the war. I like to think we will take our child to that park one day.

The weather here is a far cry from the beautiful weather of that day. It's cold here, and we spend all day out in it, training and marching through mud, snow, and ice. Our unit has few horses, so often, we have to pull equipment by hand over ice and snow-covered roads. Thinking of you and our baby and one day coming home is what helps me get through it.

Thank you for sending a picture to my mother. I still wear the socks you sent me. I will write again soon.

Your loving husband,
Philip

The training continued through the month of March, the harsh weather finally breaking and the air becoming filled with the sweetness of spring. The few trees that hadn't been torn apart by the ravages of war were beginning to come alive with tiny green buds and, here and there, grass and small flowers could be seen sprouting up in the rutted ground. Philip could just imagine how beautiful the French countryside had been before the devastation of almost four years of war.

In early April, the men were told they were leaving Gondrecourt and going to another sector. The men were marched to a railway station, where they boarded a French troop train. Soldiers, as well as horses and mules, were loaded onto trains in other areas to make the trip to the Cantigny sector. Philip was among the 6,000 men headed there. Rumors were spreading among the men that they were to take part in a battle. Philip wondered what he would face and felt excitement mixed with fear. He thought, *am I at last to see some action? Are we men, who less than a year ago were students, farm boys, or office clerks, many having never held a rifle, ready to put our training to the test? Are we really ready to go into the trenches and fight?*

Philip stood with the men of the 16th Infantry, far to the rear of the front line, waiting for the battle to begin. The men had been in the Cantigny sector since April. They arrived after a long train ride that had taken them around Paris and through an area of beautiful French countryside that had not been touched by the war and was blooming with bright red poppies.

The lovely terrain the men had seen from the train was in stark contrast to what they found in the Cantigny sector. Although they welcomed the warming spring weather after going through a brutally cold winter, the area itself was bleak and uninviting. The site of many battles, the ground was scarred with numerous shell holes and foxholes. The area was littered with human and animal remains, as flies buzzed everywhere, and most of the vegetation had been destroyed by poison gas. The nearby village of Villers-Tournelle was deserted.

The French had previously occupied the sector but had been unable to dig proper trenches or place barbed wire due to constant enemy shelling. The Germans now occupied the ruined village of Cantigny, which overlooked them from high ground a short distance away. Philip, along with the other men of the 16th and 18th Infantries, had been the first Americans to arrive there. Using their pack shovels and bayonets and working down in the existing foxholes and shell holes, they had done their best to connect them and form rudimentary trenches while the French bombarded the German stronghold with heavy artillery. Even with this, it remained dangerous work that exposed them to German snipers, causing a number of casualties.

When they weren't digging trenches, they took shelter in the buildings in Villes-Tournelle, where they worked hard building trench ladders, loading barbed wire, ammunition, water, and medical supplies onto supply wagons, and sometimes helping to prepare food for the men.

On May 3, the 18th infantry, having taken shelter in the village for the night, was assailed with artillery fired mustard gas shells, killing or injuring hundreds of the men. Philip, who had himself spent time in these same buildings, could now only think, *On another night, that might have been me!*

As the men made the necessary improvements to the battlefront, plans had been underway for what was to be the first battle of the war fought by American soldiers under American leadership. The plan was to storm the German-occupied village of Cantigny and regain some of the territory the Germans had taken in their spring offensive.

May 28th, the day of the battle, had finally arrived, and the men of Philip's unit stood in the predawn darkness, nervously talking and smoking. Their job would be to protect the rear and prevent outflanking should there be a counterattack. They would also serve as replacements on the front line should they be needed. The day dawned with a heavy mist, and as they looked up at the sky, they saw aeroplanes and a balloon. Then began the thundering booms of heavy artillery, which lasted for one full hour before 75 French tanks came from behind the men and rolled by as they moved toward the American line. Although he lost sight of the tanks, Philip knew the men of the 28th and 27th Infantry would go over the top of their trenches and follow them across no man's land in the face of German fire from the village.

The battle went on all morning. Philip spent part of this time helping to carry supplies to the trenches and transporting wounded men to the medics station. He knew how to drive a horse-drawn wagon, having done this while growing up on the farm in Michigan, and was given the job after another driver was injured. Throughout the morning, there was constant noise from machine guns, rifles, and artillery. The sound was deafening, and the air was filled with smoke from gunfire and flamethrowers. Many of the soldiers he transported were badly injured, and Philip thought that some looked like they were near death. Being in the midst of it all was frightening and disorienting. This was Philip's first real taste of war, and nothing at Camp Syracuse had prepared him for it. He just tried to keep his mind on doing his job and staying alive.

By early afternoon, word was received that the village of Cantigny had been overtaken, and the German soldiers who were still alive were taken as prisoners. The Americans had accomplished their mission and, although they had suffered many casualties, had proven their worth as an army. Philip was just grateful to have come through it alive and uninjured.

CHAPTER 13

June 5, 1918

Dear Doris,

I took part in my first battle. I can't tell you where, but you will probably read about it in the newspapers if you haven't already done so because I know of at least one reporter who was here. We lost men, but I came through it without a scratch. I was in the rear, most of the time, but spent part of the time carrying supplies to the front-line trench.

Some German soldiers were captured, and we were assigned to watch a few of them for a while before they were taken off somewhere for detainment. They were mostly young boys; some looked no more than 15 or 16. They looked pretty scared but, after a while, realized we didn't want to hurt them. Some spoke English, and a few of our men knew some German, so we were able to talk to them a little. Some said they didn't think the war had much to do with them and they were glad to now be out of it. Mostly they wanted to know about what it's like to live in America, with a couple of them saying they hoped to go there someday.

I suppose you are now getting ready to welcome our baby into the world. Please write to me as soon as he or she is born. I'll be eagerly awaiting the news. Please know that I love you and think of you every day.

I am doing my best to get through this war and come home to you and start our life together with our child.

Your loving husband,
Philip

June 10, 1918

Dear Charlie,
I have now seen action, having been part of a battle, and I can tell you firsthand how awful war is. You just don't know what it's really like until you've been a part of it. I can't tell you what battle or where we are.

You may have read about it in the newspaper. I was mostly in the rear, but did spend part of the time hauling supplies to the front line trench and bringing back wounded men. There was noise and confusion everywhere, and I have to admit I've never been so scared in my life. After things quieted down, we had to bury the dead. Some had been blown apart by machine guns and were unrecognizable. There were bodies everywhere, in the trench and in the field. We mostly buried them in shallow graves right about where they fell, along with identification tags, and marked the graves as best we could. The sergeant said that the plan is that after the war is over, they will be dug up and given proper burial. I felt sad thinking of these men, buried in a foreign country so far from home.

So far, I'm still alive and no worse for the wear. We are continuing with training, drilling and practicing trench warfare every day. When we aren't doing that, there is always work to do. I am exhausted. They haven't told us where we will go next.

Please give Mother my love and tell her I'll write to her soon.

Your brother,
Phil

There were counterattacks from the Germans for the next several days as they tried to retake the village, but finally, the area was secured, and the action moved further north. There was the business of burying the dead, and Philip took part in it, sometimes working side-by-side with Joe Kowalski. It was grim work, with bodies sometimes being blown into several pieces. There were dead animals as well – horses and a few dogs. Philip thought about Spike, who had been left behind at Gondrecourt. He thought, *Well, he's a survivor and has undoubtedly found a new group of men to befriend.*

The Americans stayed in the Cantigny sector for the next several weeks, continuing to sharpen their trench warfare skills. During this time, they were subject to enemy raids but also conducted several successful raids themselves. In the middle of July, things quieted down enough for the division to leave the area to the French. They were engaged in preparations for the move when mail came in, and Philip received a letter from Doris.

June 25, 1918

Dear Philip,

I am writing this from the confines of my bed. Our daughter was born two days ago, on June 23. She is a beautiful baby who I think looks a lot like you. She has sweet pink cheeks and lovely blue eyes. I have named her Arnette Louise and I hope you will approve of the name.

Arnette is a name I read in a book and liked it. I don't think my mother likes the name very much as she keeps suggesting others – Elizabeth for my Bowman grandmother and then Nellie for your mother. I think those names are somewhat old-fashioned and want our baby to have a more modern name. I did give her my mother's name, Louise, as a middle name.

I'm feeling fine and recovering well from the birth. The midwife said both Arnette and I are healthy. Arnette is a very good baby who sleeps most of the time between her feedings. We are now having nice, warm weather and I hope to soon be able to sit on the porch with her.

My mother said as soon as we can, we will have a photographer come and take a photograph of Arnette. When we do, I'll send you one so you can see what she looks like, I will end now as my father is here to pick up the letter and take it directly to the post office.

With love and kisses from your wife and daughter,
Doris and Arnette

Philip smiled as he read the letter. They hadn't really had much chance to discuss names for the baby, but he thought Arnette was a nice enough name. He smiled as he read and thought, *It's just like Doris to choose something different, but whatever she likes is just fine with me.* He then shouted out to Joe, along with several other men who were nearby, "Hey, I'm now a father. I have a new baby girl!"

Rousing cheers rose from the men, and all congratulated him. Some of them had known about the expected baby and had been waiting for this news. Joe had recently come into possession of a bottle of wine and had stashed it away in anticipation of this occasion. It was now opened and passed around among the men in the group.

Several other men were within earshot and rushed over to see what the excitement was about. The bottle was passed among them as well and was soon empty. Other bottles then appeared, and an impromptu party ensued, bringing about a brief respite from the death and devastation of the war. Having just survived their first battle, the men would soon be facing another, and this small celebration was a welcome distraction.

July 10, 1918

Dear Doris,
This will be a short letter as we are packing up to leave for a new

area, they haven't told us where. I didn't have any stamps, but was able to borrow one from my friend, Joe. I wanted to get a letter off to you before we leave as I don't know when I will have another chance to write.

I was happy to get your news about the baby and glad you are recovering from the birth and you and the baby are both in good health. I think Arnette is a very pretty name and I'm sure she is very pretty as well, although I hope she will turn out to look more like you!

Please do send me a photograph of Arnette when you have one. I love you very much and send kisses to both of you.

Your loving husband,
Philip

Two days later, the division was on the road, headed for Soissons, where they would join the French in a battle that would begin to turn the tide for the Allies and, eventually, bring about the end of the war.

The July weather was hot as the men made the long march from Cantigny to Soissons, carrying their heavy packs on their backs. They marched over rutted roads and through ruined fields full of shell holes and broken-down vegetation. They started out soon after dawn and walked all day, horses and mules pulling supply wagons and artillery behind them.

Late in the morning, the sergeant called out, "Company halt! Fall out for a 15-minute break and smoke if you got 'em.'"

Philip had been marching alongside Joe Kowalski and the two sat and drank water from their canteens and smoked. Philip was deep in thought, wondering what they would face in Soissons. He said, "I keep seeing all those blown-apart bodies and remembering the horrible stench. I can still smell it!"

Joe said, "I know. I think about that, too, and wonder if I'll end up like that."

Philip said, "I just want to stay alive and get home to Doris and our baby."

Joe said, "Well, we all want that, to stay alive, that is."

Philip then asked, "Have you heard from Anne?"

"Yes, I got a letter from her a few days ago. Things are the same."

Philip said, "Well, I think you should write and tell her you want to marry her, no matter what. You'll find a way."

Joe said, "Maybe I will."

Not long after that, the sergeant called out, "Break over. Form up on me. Forward March."

They then continued on toward Soissons, reaching the billeting area early that evening. The mess wagon arrived and they ate supper of canned corned beef and bread. There was work to do. Wagons had to be unloaded, and the animals tended to. Finally, exhausted from a full day of marching in the heat, Philip lay down on the ground for the night. It was a clear, starry night, and as he looked up at the sky, he thought of Doris, far away across the ocean. He thought *I wonder if she will look up and see these same stars.* As he fell asleep, he could hear the distant sounds of gunfire coming from the front lines.

CHAPTER 14

It was still dark as Philip and the other men of his division moved toward the battle line. The past few days had been filled with tension and confusion. They had remained at the billeting area, several kilometers to the rear of the battlefront, continuing to prepare weaponry and other supplies for the coming battle, which they were told little about. There appeared to be chaos as units continued to arrive and were given orders by the French, who were in charge of the operation. Their own commanding officers were late to arrive, and they later learned that congestion on the approaching roads had caused serious traffic jams and delays.

Finally, on July 17th, the men were given orders to move toward the battleground. They had walked all night, finding their way through dark woods. A severe thunderstorm had broken out, turning the ground into a sea of mud, which they slogged through, finally reaching the trenches before dawn on July 18th.

The battle began with the first wave advancing toward the German lines while Philip, wet and exhausted, was assigned to one of the reserve trenches at the rear. The trench was filled with water from the previous day's rain and smelled of an overflowing latrine. The sides of the trench were reinforced with sandbags and the men worked at shoring these up. They worked two hours on and four hours off and were told to try and sleep during their time off to be rested for their time in battle. As there was no place to lie down, Philip crouched down in the driest spot he could find and slept for a time. All during the day, the deafening sounds of cannons and gunfire were heard.

Things quieted down somewhat at nightfall. They learned that the first wave of men had been relatively successful. Although they had suffered heavy losses, they had penetrated the German-held territory and advanced about a kilometer. Sometime after midnight, Philip had been ordered out of the reserve trench. Rifles loaded and bayonets fixed, the men headed to the new front line, established by the men of the first wave on the previous day. The line of men was huge, composed of French, British, and Moroccan troops, as well as several American divisions, the 16th Infantry among them.

At 0435, there was the thundering of artillery, and tanks began rumbling forward, followed by the men of the infantry. The air became filled with bullets from machine guns and rifles. There was constant booming from artillery being fired by both sides. The noise was ear-splitting, making it impossible to speak. All around him, Philip saw men dropping but, though terrified, he kept advancing, firing his rifle when he caught sight of enemy soldiers. If a man looked like he was wounded but still alive, he shouted out for the medics, who would eventually appear with a stretcher and carry the man back to the rear.

As Philip moved forward, he felt a sudden burst of pain in his right hand, nearly causing him to drop his rifle. He found he was unable to purposefully move his fingers and, looking at his hand, saw it was covered with blood. Not knowing what he should do, he saw a large shell hole to one side and dropped down into it. When he examined his hand, he saw that there was a large hole in it.

He heard a voice in his ear, "What's the problem, soldier?"

Philip looked up and recognized his sergeant, who was crouching beside him. "I don't think I can shoot," he said as he held up his right hand, which was bleeding profusely.

The sergeant nodded. "Can you walk?" he asked.

"Yes, I'm sure I can walk," Philip answered.

"You need to go back and have the medics attend to that hand," the sergeant said, pointing to the rear. "Now go."

After the sergeant helped him out of the shell hole, Philip ran back to the line, keeping his head down until he reached one of the trenches.

He was pulled down and then heard another soldier say, "This man is injured. Take him back to the medics."

Philip was then led through the maze of trenches to the medic's station at the rear.

A doctor there examined his hand and said, "This hand has been shot through. He needs to go to the base hospital."

The doctor applied a thick field dressing to Philip's hand to try to stanch the flow of blood, and Philip was directed to an ambulance, along with other wounded men, some with severe injuries and others who were walking wounded, like himself.

After a long ride over rough roads, the ambulance arrived at the base hospital #27. When Philip reached the hospital, he was immediately stripped of all his clothes and placed in a vat of hot water to bathe and delouse him. He was then given clean pajamas and placed on a stretcher in a waiting area among men with all manner of injuries. Next to him was a man who had had part of his face blown off. Some men were missing limbs, and others looked as if they were near death. The doctors and nurses moved purposefully around the room, attending to the worst cases first.

Philip's hand was examined and then carefully cleaned. He was then taken to the operating theater, where a mask was placed over his face. When he awoke, he was in a bed in a large ward, and his right hand was tightly bandaged and painful.

A nurse was at his bedside and, smiling at him, said, "I see you are awake. You had a nasty machine gun hole in your hand, but the doctor cleaned it out and sewed it up. Are you in pain?"

Philip said, "My hand hurts, but I'm okay."

The nurse then said, "I'll bring you some soup," and went off to fetch it.

She soon returned with a bowl of hot soup along with some medicine to help relieve his pain. Philip had to eat with his left hand, but he managed. He realized he was starving, not having eaten in many hours, and the soup tasted delicious. After he ate, he lay back on the bed. In spite of the pain in his hand, he felt the most comfortable he had in months. Not having been able to properly bathe in weeks, he luxuriated in the cleanliness. Exhausted, he fell into a deep sleep.

July 25, 1918

Dear Doris,
I'm writing this from the hospital. I was shot in my hand on July 19 and brought here to Base Hospital #27, where the doctors stitched it up. They are still worried about infection, but a nurse told me it looks like it is healing well. By the time you get this, I may already be back at the front.

A very nice woman from the Red Cross is writing this letter for me as my right hand has a large bandage on it, making it hard for me to write. They are taking very good care of me here. I'm comfortable and getting good food to eat. I hope you and Arnette are both doing well. Please write to my mother and tell her that I'm in the hospital but expected to completely recover.

Your loving husband,
Philip

The nurse removed the bandage from Philip's hand and carefully examined it. It had been two weeks since his injury and the redness and swelling in his hand had greatly decreased, as well as the pain. A nurse came once a day to change his dressing and always seemed to be pleased with the way it was healing. She now said, "The doctor was worried about infection because your wound was quite dirty, but, so far, there are no signs of it, and your hand is healing up very well."

After three weeks in the hospital, the stitches were removed from Philip's hand, and the doctor pronounced him completely healed and fit to go back to the front. Just before he left, he received some mail that had been forwarded to the hospital. One of the letters was from Doris, who wrote:

July 15, 1918

Dear Philip,

I think of you all the time and hope you are safe. We read about the war in the newspapers every day. They report that our American soldiers are making good gains toward winning the war, and there are great hopes it will soon be brought to an end. They always list the local men who have been killed or wounded, and I think of you over there in harm's way and hope you are alright.

Arnette and I are doing fine. She is now three weeks old and appears to be very healthy. My mother loves her and fusses over her a great deal.

Helen Shore stopped over to see me this week. She brought a pink hat her mother had made for Arnette and spent some time holding her. Helen is now attending college, taking a stenography course. When she finishes her course of study, she plans to seek employment at one of the downtown businesses. Helen is truly a modern woman! She has even learned to drive a motorcar. I have spoken to my father about teaching me to drive as well.

I miss you and love you very much. I hope and pray that this war will soon come to an end and that you will return to me.

Your loving wife,
Doris

Philip received his orders to return to the front lines and, wearing a clean uniform, he said goodbye to the doctors and nurses and made the long ride back to the front. He thought about Doris. *Well, by now, she will have gotten my letter and know about my injury, but that I'm alright.* He looked at his hand, which had a scar and was still somewhat stiff and swollen but was improving every day. He squeezed it into a tight fist and then opened it. He was now able to move all his fingers without difficulty.

He had wondered about Joe and the other men in his company. He had asked at the hospital and had been told by incoming men that the battle at Soissons had ended, but details were sparse. He was eager to get back among the men and hear a full report. When he reached the billeting area, he sought out Joe, who was glad to see him. The battle had been a bloody one with heavy losses among the allies but had had a successful outcome. The army had made significant gains in territory and destroyed a portion of a major rail line. With their supply line cut off, the Germans had been forced to withdraw from the area.

Joe reported on some of the men they knew who had been killed in the action and others who were badly injured. Joe, himself, had come through the battle completely unharmed. Philip showed him his hand. "It's getting better every day," he said.

That night, the two men sat under the stars, smoking and talking, as was their habit. They talked, among other things, about home and family. Joe said, "I finally took up your suggestion and wrote to Anne about getting married. After you were hurt and then Sam and Paul were killed, I thought about how lucky I would be if I made it through this war alive. I told Anne that if I made it home in one piece, I would do whatever I had to do to be with her, even if it means going against my family."

"I suppose it's too soon to have heard back from her," Philip said.

"Yes, you're right. I haven't heard yet, but I'm hoping that when I do, she will agree."

Philip talked about Doris. He said, "I think she's a little jealous of her friend who is now going to college and has learned to drive a motorcar." I think staying home with her parents every day and caring for a baby must be hard for her. She likes to have fun."

Joe said, "She's probably just lonely. She misses you."

Philip said, "I think you are right. Things will be much better when I'm home, and we can really start our life together." Still, he wondered if Doris ever had regrets about marrying him. Everything had happened so fast. He knew she loved him but wondered if she wished she could be a "modern woman" like Helen. *When I get home, I'll work hard to give her the best life I can. She will have no reasons for any regrets.*

CHAPTER 15

August 12, 1918

Dear Doris,
I am now out of the hospital and back at the front. My hand has healed well. The doctors did a good job of fixing it, and I can move all my fingers. It's still a little stiff and sore, but it's getting better every day. I was glad to see my good friend Joe, who made it through the battle without injury. He gave me some bad news about two of our friends who didn't make it. One of them was a fellow I knew from Camp Syracuse. He was a nice guy – young like most of us. I can't believe he's gone. I think about Andy Wise a lot and wonder where he is and if he is still alive. I hope so.

I'm glad you still see Helen. I'll always remember how she and Andy stood up for us when we were married and our supper at the Cobblestone Inn. What a wonderful night that was. It now seems like so long ago.

I got your last letter just before I left the hospital, and I'm glad you and Arnette are doing well. I hope you will be able to have a picture taken of Arnette soon. I'm eager to get a look at my daughter. I'm going to end now. I have to write a letter to my mother. I'll write again soon. Love and kisses to you and Arnette.

Your loving husband,
Philip

Over the next several days, Philip received several letters from home:

Doris wrote:
August 10, 1918

Dear Philip,
I got the letter you wrote from the hospital and hope you are recovering from your injury. I have called the Syracuse newspaper and told them about your injury. I was told that it will be reported in the newspaper along with reports of other local men who have been killed or wounded. I read the war casualty lists whenever they appear and have sometimes seen the name of a boy I knew from school or church. I haven't yet seen Andy Wise's name and hope, as I know you do, that I don't.

Reading the war news and hearing about your injury only serves to remind me about the great danger you are in every day. Please do try to be as careful as you can. I so much want you to come back to Arnette and me. I think of you every day and go to sleep thinking about you at night. You are always in my dreams. I long to be back in your arms and feel your kisses.

I wrote to your mother, as you asked, and told her about your injured hand and also that you expected to make a complete recovery.

Your loving wife,
Doris

Nellie wrote:
August 12, 1918

Dear Son,
I got a letter from Doris telling me about your wounded hand. She said you were hit by a bullet during a battle and were in a hospital but that you expected to completely recover. I hope that is true and that you are now well.

I worry about you every day. Your stepfather sometimes brings the newspaper home, and we read about the war. We have read and heard in church of local men who have died in the war. Rev. Fellows says prayers for our boys at the front every week.

It's raining today, and I'm inside catching up on some housework. We've been busy in the garden as a lot of the crops are coming in and need to be picked and taken to market. Claude has tried to hire some extra help but, with so many men off fighting in the war, he hasn't had any luck.

Doris told me she liked the booties I made and sent to the baby, Arnette. She said the baby is pretty and looks a lot like you. I hope one of these days I will be able to see her. I'll sign off for now. Charlie is going to write a few lines and put them in with this letter. He's a big help to us on the farm. I don't know what we would do without him. Please stay as safe as you can and come home to us.

With love,
Mother

Charlie wrote:

Dear Phil,
We heard all about your bullet wound, and I'm glad you are all right. We miss you here on the farm. As you know, this is our busy season, with a lot of the crops coming in. Claude is working me hard, as usual, but I don't really mind. Someone has to do it.

It must be exciting to be over there and be part of the action. I'm 18 now and have thought about joining the Army, but Mother doesn't want me to. She said I'm needed here on the farm and, besides, she worries about losing us both. So, for now, I'll wait and see what happens. If the war goes on much longer, I may think about signing up, but hope it won't last too much longer. The newspapers say that our American soldiers have won some battles, so, hopefully, we can finally beat the Germans.

I played my violin in church last Sunday, and after the service, a few people came up and talked to me. Some asked about you. It's been so long since we've seen you. Hope you will be home soon.

Your brother,
Charlie

There were other letters. One was from his grandparents and there were two from ladies who attended his church. Reading the letters made him think of home, about the farm, and growing up in Michigan. At one time, his only thoughts had been of leaving there and getting away from the farm, but now he remembered the good times they had had as a family. The hot, sunny weather they were now having in France reminded him of warm Michigan summers. He remembered all the fun he and Charlie had had running through the fields and woods and climbing trees.

He also thought about his grandparents' house on the hill on South Marshall Avenue and pictured his small room at the top of the winding staircase. He remembered meals around the big dining room table and the good food his grandmother had prepared. He had always been close to his maternal Grandparents, Frank and Angeline Smith, and missed them terribly. He realized it had been over a year since he had last seen them.

His thoughts also drifted back to this time last summer when he and Doris had been newly married and had spent a day at Long Branch Park. He remembered all the fun they had had. He felt in his pocket for the small drawing of Doris that he always carried. He'd had it in his pocket when he went to the hospital, but someone must have taken it out, as one of the nurses had returned it to him after he had awoken from his surgery. He unfolded it now and smiled as he looked at it.

It had now been nine months since he had left camp Syracuse. When he thought of all that had happened, it seemed like much longer. He had traveled across the ocean to another country, gone through a hard winter of training, and been in two battles. He'd been injured but was still alive. He wondered what now lay ahead. This sector had quieted down, but they could hear distant gunfire. The war was still going on.

Philip wondered what was coming next, and he just wanted to go home. He missed Doris and wanted to be with her and hold their baby. He'd already missed two months of Arnette's life and wondered how much more he would miss. He knew, however, that he was doing something important and didn't really have regrets about signing up. When the war was finally won, the world would be a safer place, and the French people would have their country back.

There was always work to be done and the men kept busy. There were rumors that they would be on the move before long, headed to another sector and another battle, but they wouldn't know for sure until orders came.

The orders finally came in early September and they began packing up to move.

CHAPTER 16

It feels like we've been walking forever, Philip thought as he trudged along in the dark. In fact, they had been walking for almost a week. He felt exhausted and chilled to the bone as he walked along with Joe, his pack weighing heavily on his back.

The weather isn't making it any easier. Is it ever going to stop raining?

His thoughts took him back to the long hikes he took from Camp Syracuse when he was training to be a soldier. The warm summer weather had been pleasant then and, although he and his fellow recruits had all complained, those hikes now seemed like a school sporting event compared to what he was now experiencing. Looking back, he realized he'd had no idea what real war would be like.

They were progressing toward another battlefront – one that the men had been told little about, except the intent was to take the German army by surprise. Due to this, troop movement took place mostly at night. They moved stealthily along in the dark, the roads teeming with men, animals, and equipment. It had rained almost constantly, and the roads became seas of mud in which the men were often ankle-deep. Sometimes, the equipment became mired in the mud, and the men had to get behind a wagon or truck and push it out. Philip slipped and fell during one of these operations, his whole body becoming mud-covered.

The army stayed off the roads during the day for fear of

being spotted by aerial reconnaissance and took shelter where they could. Sometimes, he and Joe had been able to stay in deserted farm buildings, but most days, they hid in the woods, finding shelter as best they could under trees. Usually, the trees afforded little protection, many having been torn to shreds by guns and artillery, but on this day, they were fortunate to be in an especially thick growth of trees, and the rain had temporarily stopped.

Philip used the opportunity to try to dry off as much as he could. He was wearing the socks that Doris had sent him, and when he removed his boots, saw that they had leaked and the socks were sodden and caked with mud. He had another pair in his pack, so he removed the ones he had been wearing and hung them on low-hanging branches. He stared at his feet. They looked similar to the plucked chickens he had helped butcher on the farm – cold and pale. He rubbed them in an attempt to warm them, and their color improved, but they felt unbelievably sore. He hung some of his clothes on branches, hoping to dry them as much as possible. He didn't know when he might be able to truly wash them. It sounded like they would be busy during the coming days.

Philip's unit arrived at the St. Mihiel salient – a German stronghold that the French and American armies were hoping to reduce – on September 11th. Trenches had been dug, but the troops had not yet occupied them, as they were hoping to take the Germans by surprise. The rain continued off and on; feeling exhausted, cold, wet, hungry, and totally wretched, Philip was immediately put to work unloading supplies and carrying ammunition into the trenches. His whole body hurt, and he felt like the chill and dampness had permeated his bones. There was nowhere to take shelter, and he took his supper break standing out in the open in the continuing drizzle. The trucks carrying the food were late in arriving and, when they finally did come, the food tasted like mud. Shivering with the cold, he felt like he would never be warm again.

Late that night, the men began moving into the trenches.

At exactly 1 am on September 12, the cannon barrage began. Thousands of cannons fired simultaneously, lighting up the sky. Nearly deafened by the thundering booms, the frightened men in the trenches stared around them in amazement as the surrounding landscape became as bright as day. This barrage continued for several hours until, at 5 AM, tanks began rolling forward. A whistle blew, and the first wave of men climbed up wooden ladders and "over the top" in the drizzling rain and mist. Clutching their rifles, they followed the tanks across "no man's land" toward the German barbed wire.

Shivering with the cold, Philip watched the whole thing unfold in frightened fascination from his place in one of the rear trenches. He would move forward and join the battle as needed. He remembered this last battle at Soissons and how terrifying it had been to be in the midst of a charging army – the noise and confusion and wondering if he would live through it. He had come out of it with only a wounded hand but wondered if he would be as lucky this time.

Will I still be alive tomorrow? he wondered. *Will I ever see Doris again or hold our daughter?*

He was overwhelmed by a cold feeling of dread, unlike anything he had ever known. He looked over at Joe and saw him staring straight ahead, his thoughts unknown.

Philip never became part of the conflict. He later learned that the Germans had been in the process of evacuating St. Mihiel, and the American army was able to advance on the town the second day of the battle, continuing south and west, restoring miles of French territory and opening up rail and water transportation that had been closed down for months. Most of the Germans had managed to escape, taking much of their equipment, but a great many prisoners were taken and hundreds of guns captured. The operation was considered a great success, and casualties were far fewer than had been expected.

He wondered what would come next. There were rumors that

the war might be coming to an end before too much longer. The endless supply of strong, young men provided by the American army was starting to make a difference, and loss of life and the deprivation caused by four years of war were starting to take their toll on the German army.

If I can just stay alive a little longer, I may make it home after all, Philip thought.

September 18, 1918

Dear Doris,

I have just been through another big battle. I can't write much about it except to say that our army was able to free up an area that the Germans had occupied since early in the war. I was lucky and stayed in the rear trenches, never making it up to the front battle line before the operation ended. Even though I wasn't on the front lines, I still felt what I did was important, and I was proud to be there and do my share. The operation was a great success, and I suppose you will read about it in the papers. Our General, along with some French officers, visited a little town that was taken from the Germans the night of that battle and found that the people living there were mostly older people, women, and children. The town had been under German occupation since the beginning of the war, and the citizens hadn't even known that the Americans were in France.

I hope you and our baby, Arnette, are doing well. I suppose Arnette is growing every day. I miss you both so much, and a day never goes by that you are not in my thoughts. I hope your parents are well. You said in your last letter that your father had been sick and I hope he has recovered. There have been a few cases of influenza in our company, the men needing to go to the field hospital. They don't want the rest of us to be infected with it. I'm trying to be very careful not to get sick.

I don't know what will happen next or where we will go. I'm just hoping that the war will end soon and I can come home to you.

Your faithful husband,
Philip

Philip and Joe sat in the damp gloom, smoking and talking.

"I can't believe we made it through another one, and we're both still alive," Joe said.

"I wonder how much longer our luck can hold out," said Philip.

"There are rumors that another big battle is coming," said Joe. "I'm going to write down my parents' names and address and give it to you. If anything happens to me, would you write to them about how you knew me and how we fought together? I think they would like to hear that."

"What about Anne?" Philip asked.

"Yes, I'll give you hers as well," said Joe.

"OK, I'll do the same," said Philip. "I'll give you Doris's address."

The two men exchanged addresses, and within a few days, they were on the move again, heading toward a battle that would end the war for Philip and cause him to lose all contact with Joe.

CHAPTER 17

Philip heard the bells from his hospital bed.

He had to stop and think, *Is it Sunday?*

He didn't think so, but he sometimes lost track of the days, one being pretty much like another here in the hospital. They were definitely church bells; he knew that for sure. He had heard them many times, ringing out from the churches of nearby towns, but this day, they seemed louder, and there were many more than usual.

He looked around the ward filled with recovering men lying on hospital beds or sitting up in wheelchairs. Others appeared puzzled as well, and he got up and walked to a window but saw nothing outside but the clear fall day. The bells seemed to be coming from everywhere. He knew the louder ones came from the churches in nearby Bulcy and Mesves-sur-Loire, but more distant ones could also be heard, ringing out from afar and rolling across distant fields and hills before reaching his room in the huge army hospital.

He then heard a commotion outside the door to the ward and, as the occupants in the room looked toward the doorway, a nurse rushed in.

"It's over!" she said. "We just heard it on the radio. The armistice was signed at eleven o'clock. The war is over!"

There were cheers and shouts from around the room as Philip sat in stunned silence.

Over? he thought. Is it really over?

"What's today's date ?" he asked the nurse after she entered the room.

"It's the eleventh," she said. "November 11, 1918."

He had lost track of the time he had spent at Base Hospital #50 recovering from a gas attack. He had now been in France for almost a year. His mind took him back to November 20th of last year when he had seen Doris for the last time, waving goodbye to her as he boarded the train in Syracuse. So much has happened since! The many hours of training and marching in all kinds of weather. The four battles he had been through. The hand wound that had sent him to the hospital for three weeks. He thought about living through days of fear, hunger, and all kinds of physical discomfort, wondering the whole time if he would live to return home to his wife and baby. And now it was over. The Great War had ended.

It had been just over a month since he had been gassed in the Argonne Forest on one of the first days of that battle. After walking the sixty miles from St. Mihiel, his company had entered the forest in a state of disorganized confusion. The roads leading to the forest had been jammed with men and equipment, causing major tie-ups and delays as traffic sometimes came to a complete stop. Influenza had been spreading through the company and, although Philip had so far managed to avoid it, several men had been ill with it, further complicating things.

The men had been told that this was to be an important mission that could eventually lead to a final defeat of the Germans. The goal had been to travel north through the forest, along the Meusse River, and reach the little village of Fleville, which was held by the Germans. After liberating the village, the plan was to push north to Sedan. The men had entered a dugout and, after maneuvering through a long tunnel, had jumped from their foxholes into a thick yellow haze.

Gas! Philip had immediately thought.

The men had been taught about the dangers and effects of gas, and it was one of the things he feared the most, but this was the first time he had actually experienced it. He had been wearing his gas mask, but a yellow film clouded the lens, partially obscuring his vision. He used his arm to wipe it off as best he could to try and clear it. He felt breathless and panicked as he stumbled forward over the uneven ground, falling and then getting back up. He looked down at his rain-soaked clothes and saw that they were covered with yellow residue. He looked around for Joe but didn't see him. Joe had been among the group of men who had entered the forest but was now nowhere to be seen, and Philip hoped he was okay. As he continued forward, he was approached by someone who pointed him to the rear.

"Go that way, soldier," the man said. "Someone will take you to the field hospital."

Philip did as he was instructed and eventually found himself outside the crowded field hospital, some distance from the rear of the front. A large tent had been put up, and inside it were men being treated for battle wounds, as well as several who were ill with influenza. Philip was propelled toward a large truck near the tent and men who were wearing protective clothing and masks shouted instructions at him as they began removing his clothes. The truck held a large water boiler and three or four shower heads. Philip was pushed under the showers and cleaned off. After the shower, his nose and mouth were sprayed with bicarbonate of soda before he was given clean clothes and directed into the tent hospital. Once in the tent, he was offered food and water. He took a few sips of water but declined any food. He wasn't hungry and felt as if he might vomit. He itched all over and found it hard to breathe.

"My throat feels like it's closing up," he said.

He was instructed to lie down, and a metal mask with a menthol-soaked cloth was placed over his face. Breathing the cool solution gave him some relief, but he continued to feel ill and finally vomited.

It was decided to keep him at the field hospital overnight for observation. During the night, he woke up unable to breathe, and emergency oxygen was delivered. The next day, he was transported by train to Base Hospital #50, a huge complex of prefab buildings between the towns of Mesves-sur-Loire and Bulcy, about 150 miles south of Paris.

Over the past month, Philip had been given what was the standard treatment for gas injuries. At regular intervals, he was taken to a room with a large container of oxygen and a mask was placed over his face, allowing him to inhale the oxygen. This gave him temporary relief from the feeling of breathlessness he often experienced, but this feeling would inevitably return after the treatment was over. Night times were the worst, and he would awaken unable to breathe and give a choked call to the nurse, who would raise his head on pillows and try to calm him. Sometimes, he would be given a sedative to help him sleep. As time went by, those episodes had been less frequent, although he still coughed and became short of breath after even moderate exertion. He was receiving the oxygen treatments less frequently now and supposed they would end soon. He had not yet been told when he could return to his unit and the front, but he supposed now that the war had ended, he probably wouldn't be going back.

Maybe I'll just be sent home, he thought. *There doesn't seem to be any reason to keep me here now.*

He wondered about Joe and the others in his unit. He hadn't been able to learn anything, but the hospital was huge with men from all over. He thought there was probably a good chance that he wouldn't see any of them again, and the idea of not being able to say goodbye to Joe and some of his other friends made him sad, even though the idea of going home filled him with happiness. He would be reunited with Doris and, at last, be able to hold his baby daughter.

His mail had finally caught up with him, and there were several letters from home: one from Charlie, one from his mother, and two from Doris.

Doris wrote:
October 10, 1918

Dear Philip,
I received two letters from you this week and, as usual, felt a sense of relief reading your words and knowing you were at least still alive and well when the letters were written. My father finally recovered from the stomach ailment that kept him down for several days and has returned to work. My mother is now very ill with a fever and a bad cough. A nurse came to see her yesterday and said she has influenza, which is going around here. A lot of people are ill with it, many hospitalized. According to the newspapers, it seems to have started at Camp Syracuse and has now spread throughout the city. This week, Mayor Stone ordered schools and churches to close, along with many other public places. All public meetings are now forbidden, and people are being told to stay inside.

Mother has been confined to her bedroom, and I'm caring for her as best I can. The nurse gave me a gauze mask and I wear it whenever I go into her room. So far, Arnette and I remain healthy, and I hope that continues. Whenever I can, I take Arnette out for a walk in her carriage; as they say, it is good to be out in the fresh, open air.

We continue to get the daily newspaper and I'm able to read the news of the war. I always read through the casualty lists, looking for names I might know, and I'm afraid I have some terrible news for you. Listed among those killed in action was Lawrence Andrew Wise of Liverpool. Survivors listed were his parents and sister. I am so sorry to have to give you that news but know you would want to know. Andy was such a good friend to you – to us both, really – standing up for us at our marriage and all. That seems so long ago now. I liked Andy a lot and feel so sorry that he is gone.

I'm grateful that you have so far managed to stay alive and can only hope for the war to end soon. I look forward to the day when you will be back in my arms.

Your loving wife,
Doris

Within a few days of the war's end, Philip was deemed recovered enough to be released from the hospital and fit for travel, although not well enough to return to his unit. He was ordered to St. Nazaire where he was to await orders for transport home. He soon found himself on a train crowded with other soldiers and, as he rode along, looking out the windows as the French countryside rolled by, he thought of all that had happened in the past year.

It was hard to believe the war was finally over, and he would soon be able to go home. Just one month ago, he'd had no idea of that happening anytime soon and now here he was, headed home after what seemed to him like an abrupt end to a war he thought would never end. He thought about Andy Wise, now lying in a cold grave far from home. He had to hold back tears as he thought about the smiling young man who had been such a good friend to him. He remembered the times they had shared at training camp, both good and bad, many funny, and the plans they had made to meet up again after the war was over.

Well, that won't be happening now, he thought sadly. He cried out in his mind, *Andy, I can't believe you are gone!*

He wondered how Andy had died. Maybe he was cut down by machine guns while running across no man's land or hit by a sniper bullet as he huddled in a trench. He shuddered as he thought of the many men he had seen killed in these ways, bodies blown apart, sometimes beyond recognition.

He thought about Andy's parents, how proud they had been of their only son, and how nice they had been to him and Doris.

When I get back to Syracuse, I'll go and visit them, he thought. *I think Andy would like that. Well, I'm lucky to have survived,* he thought. *Many others didn't.*

His thoughts turned to Doris, and he wondered what it would be like to see her again after so long. Would they both have changed? And baby Arnette. He would finally get to see and hold her. He counted on his fingers.

She is now almost five months old, he thought.

He remembered the small celebration he had with his friends when he learned of her birth, and it now seemed so long ago.

November 18, 1918

Dear Doris,

I am here in St. Nazaire, waiting for orders to travel back to the States. The town is filled with other men, both American and British soldiers, also on their way home. The US barracks were full when I arrived, and so I was put up in a boarding house owned by a French family. The house is clean, and I have a small room upstairs. It seems strange to be sleeping in a room by myself. It has been a long time since I have done that. Madame Dubois, who is the landlady, is very nice, and the food is decent. Madame Dubois is a good cook and, even with the food shortages, manages to prepare pretty good meals for us, using vegetables stored from her summer garden and what she can buy at the market.

I'm feeling better. I still feel out of breath at times, but I think being out in the fresh air is helping me. It's getting colder, but on nice days, I sometimes sit outside and have taken a few short walks. There isn't much to do, and I have a lot of time to think, wondering what our lives will be like when we are finally together again. We've never really had a chance to live together as husband and wife, and now we will also have Arnette. I suppose I'll find some kind of job.

I don't know what. I'll talk to your father about it and see what he suggests. My year of business college should help me qualify for a job at one of the companies in Syracuse.

I'll write again as soon as I have my orders.

Your loving husband,
Philip

December 1, 1918

Dear Doris,

I have just received my orders. I'm leaving St. Nazaire on December 6th to Hoboken, New Jersey. From there, I will be posted to Camp Sherman, Ohio, where I suppose my discharge will be processed. That's all I know for now but will update you as I learn more.

The days pass by slowly here, and I just want to go home. Gradually, men are leaving and others replace them, coming here from all over France, but none from my own company that I have run into. It keeps Madame Dubois busy, keeping up with it. Her husband is an officer in the French army and has not returned. Her daughter, Marie, lives nearby and comes over to help. Marie's husband is also away at the front, and she is worried as she has not heard from him recently. She has a ten-year-old son named Pierre, who sometimes comes over on days he doesn't have school. We've talked a few times. He knows some English and between that and the little French I've learned, we have managed to talk and, a few times, taken short walks together. Just yesterday, we walked to the harbor to look at the ships.

Pierre is a nice boy who reminds me somewhat of my brother, Charlie. He likes to play football and hopes to play on a team now that the war has ended. The football in France is different from our football. It sounds more like what we call soccer. I tried to explain about our football and told him about playing on a team back when I lived in Marshall. Pierre is always interested in hearing about

America, and I tell him what I can with my limited French and what he can understand of English.

Well, it will only be a few more days, and I'll be leaving here, so this will probably be my last letter. It's hard to believe that in less than a week, my time in France will be over, and I'll be on my way home. Soon we'll be together again. I have to get a letter off to my mother. Please give my best to your parents. I'll be seeing you soon.

Your loving husband,
Philip

Philip was among the many hundreds of American soldiers on the British ship Mercury as it sailed from France on December 6, 1918 headed for home, the Great War behind them.

PART III
HOMECOMING

CHAPTER 18

The voyage across the ocean had been grueling, and Philip thought it would never end. As was the case when he had traveled to France the previous year, the ship was crowded, with the men confined to the lower decks.

Once again, many of the men became seasick due to the constant rolling and pitching of the ship, which was made worse when they hit an Atlantic storm. Many of the men were afflicted with war wounds and were in varying stages of healing, and some, like Philip, had experienced gas attacks from which they were still recovering. Added to all the misery were several cases of influenza. The men diagnosed with that illness were confined to separate areas of the ship, but Philip lived in constant fear that he would contract it.

He continued to feel short of breath most of the time, and this symptom was made worse by the conditions in the stuffy confines of the lower deck. He felt worse at night when he often awoke breathless and coughing. The men were allowed on the upper deck once or twice a day, and Philip welcomed the temporary relief that change brought. He would stand on the open deck and breathe in the clean, fresh air, not wanting to return to the stifling atmosphere of the lower quarters.

After the seemingly endless ocean voyage came the overland trip on a crowded train. There had been no way to lie down, and he'd been forced to sit up for the entire distance from the New Jersey coast to Camp Sherman, Ohio.

Once reaching the camp, the processing of so many men seemed to take forever, and all Philip could think about was finding a place where he could lie down and go to sleep. At last, he was seen by a doctor who told him he would need to spend a few days in the hospital there.

On December 20, 1919, Philip wrote:

Dear Doris,

I'm now back in the USA and here at the hospital at Camp Sherman, Ohio. The trip from France was long, but we made it. The camp doctor wanted me to spend some time here at the hospital to make sure I have completely recovered from the gas attack. They are giving me breathing treatments and telling me I'm getting better.

I expect to be cleared for discharge soon, and when I know the date, I will let you know. I hope you and Arnette are doing well. Several men came down with influenza on the trip back, but I was lucky to escape it. I'm going to get a letter off to my mother. I didn't have any writing paper or stamps, but a nice lady from the YMCA supplied me with some. I hope you have a happy Christmas. Next year we will be together.

Love,
Philip

In early January, he received a reply from Doris:

December 27, 1919

Dear Philip,
I got your letter and am so happy that you made it safely back. I'm

glad you are getting the care you need but hope you won't be in the hospital for too long. I am eagerly awaiting your return to me.

We had a quiet Christmas here. It was Arnette's first Christmas, and we celebrated as best we could, but it wasn't the same without you. I look forward to next Christmas when the three of us will be together – our little family in our own home. We had a big snowstorm here a few days ago, but today it is sunny, although very cold. I wonder what the weather is like where you are.

My father has been helping look for a place for us to live when you come home, and we found a small house for rent on Edgewood Avenue, just around the corner from where my parents live. It's a nice house and has some furniture. My parents are giving us some extra things they have, and my grandmother, Jennie, has an attic full of furniture and household goods that she can easily spare.

I will await news from you telling me when you'll be home. My mother and father send their regards and loving kisses from Arnette.

Your faithful and loving wife,
Doris.

The days passed slowly for Philip. The hospital ward was crowded, and he made friends with several of the men in nearby beds, passing the time telling and listening to others' wartime experiences. Sam, the man in the bed next to him, was suffering with a bad artillery wound he had received in the Argonne Forest – the same place Philip was gassed. His leg had become seriously infected, and Sam was often subjected to painful treatments in an attempt to heal it. Sam tried to be positive but lived in fear of losing the leg.

Thinking about Sam made Philip feel grateful.

At least I'm still in one piece, he thought.

At other times, he didn't feel as hopeful. He continued to lose his breath at night and often had nightmares about things that had happened in the war. He would sometimes awaken, not knowing where he was, and, hearing the voices of the other men, would panic, thinking he was back at the front.

Daytime was better, and the men were often visited by volunteers from the YMCA who brought them books and magazines from the camp library or spent time visiting and talking with them. Philip looked forward to his letters from Doris, who continued to write faithfully and dreamed of the time they would be reunited. He continued to be given breathing treatments but was told little about his condition or when he would be discharged from the hospital.

At last toward the end of January, he was given the news that he could expect to leave the hospital within the week to await his discharge orders.

On January 30, Philip wrote:

Dear Doris,

I'm at last out of the hospital and have received my orders. I am to be discharged on February 10th at 7 am and have been told I will be given travel pay to Battle Creek, Michigan, where I first enlisted in the Army. I can use that money to take a train to Syracuse but would like to see my mother and Charlie. I haven't seen them in such a long time.

Would it be possible for you (and Arnette) to take the train to Battle Creek and meet me there? From there, we can take a bus to the farm, or maybe one of my uncles can pick us up. I'll write to my mother as well. Please write back as soon as you get this and let me know if this plan sounds possible.

There is a telephone here at the camp, but you have to make an appointment to use it. I'll try to do that. I'll wait to hear from you, but can't wait to hold you in my arms. It has been so long.

Love from your faithful husband,
Philip

On February 4th, Doris wrote:

Dear Phllip,
I was so happy to get your letter. Yes, I will take the train to Michigan. My father drove me to the train station yesterday, and I bought a ticket to Battle Creek for February 10th. The train leaves Syracuse at 8 am and is due to arrive in Battle Creek at 5 pm the same day.

I am so excited that I'm going to see you soon. I can hardly believe that the war is over and, at last, we will be together again. I hope you'll be able to call. I am eager to hear your voice and will try to stay close to the telephone. If we don't talk, I'll see you in Battle Creek!

Your loving wife,
Doris

Philip spent his last days at Camp Sherman walking around the base. The weather was cold, but he preferred to keep busy rather than sit in the barracks. He spent part of his time visiting some of the men he knew who were still in the hospital, including Sam. Sam's leg, failing to respond to the treatments he was given, had finally been amputated, but he was maintaining a positive attitude and looking forward to his return home. Seeing him made Philip realize that, although he continued to cough and have difficulty breathing at times, he was better off than so many others.

On February 10th, after his discharge was processed, a bus drove the men to a nearby train station, and Philip boarded a train to Battle Creek, arriving there in the early afternoon. As Doris's train wasn't due to arrive until 5 pm, he had plenty of time to spare. He used the time to find a pay telephone and place a call to his uncle, who was excited to hear from him. When Philip asked his uncle if he could come to the station at 5 o'clock and then drive them to the farm, his uncle said, "I'll come now and keep you company while you wait for your bride."

His uncle arrived within an hour and treated Philip to lunch at the station cafeteria, after which they spent time catching up on family news and some of the things Philip had seen and done in France.

Philip heard the announcement that the Syracuse train had arrived, and his heart stopped. He held his breath as he watched passengers disembarking, one after another, from the train.

His mouth felt suddenly dry, and he felt a cold chill as he thought, *what if she's not on the train? Could she have somehow missed it?*

As this thought crossed his mind, he saw a small woman wearing a dark blue coat and matching hat descend the steps of the train. She looked up and down the platform and smiled as she spotted Philip standing next to his uncle. He saw her at the same moment and ran toward her. Suddenly, they were in each other's arms, both laughing, their eyes brimming over with tears of happiness.

CHAPTER 19

Philip sat staring silently out the train window as the snow-covered fields of, what was obviously, farm country rolled by. He had no idea where they were. It was hot and stuffy inside the car, and that, combined with the motion of the train, had caused him to feel sleepy and doze off for a while, so he had missed any landmarks that might have given him clues as to their location.

He felt confused on first awakening, thinking he was still in France being transported to some unknown battle, but quickly realized that he was back in the United States on his way to his new home in Syracuse, New York. He and Doris had left Battle Creek, Michigan, early that morning after spending a few days with his family, but he wasn't sure exactly how far they had traveled.

Oh well, he thought. *It really doesn't matter. If I want to know, I can always ask the conductor or another passenger.*

As he continued to look out the window, he saw that it was an overcast day – typical of this time of year. The trees were all bare, but he knew that in another month or so, they would start to sprout small spring buds.

The train was full. Among the passengers were many young men, probably, like him, recently discharged from the army and on their way home. He smiled as he looked over at Doris, sleeping quietly on the seat beside him. *She's so pretty,* he thought. He bent over and breathed in her sweet scent, her light floral perfume contrasting with the odors of engine smoke and the sweaty, un-washed bodies of the other passengers.

It was February 1919, less than a week since his discharge from the army. Doris had taken the train to Battle Creek and met him there, after which they had continued on to the farm. He had been disappointed that Doris had not brought their daughter, Arnette, but she had explained that her parents had been against the idea of taking the baby on a crowded train in the middle of winter, es-pecially with the recent influenza epidemic so fresh in everyone's mind. He knew that she was right and it was better that Arnette remain safely with her grandparents but was never-the-less disap-pointed. He was eager to meet his daughter, who was now eight months old. He knew that his mother had been disappointed as well.

Well, I'll meet her soon enough, he thought and smiled. He and Doris were finally going to begin their life together. He was hope-ful of finding a good job. The year of business college he had at-tended before enlisting in the army should help him do that. Also, his father-in-law knew a lot of people and had promised to help him secure a good position with one of the many companies in Syracuse. Doris had already found a small house not far from her parents' home where they would live.

Having spent over a month at the hospital at Camp Sherman, he continued to feel the effects of the gas attack he had experi-enced on the battlefield in France. He still had a cough and, at times, had difficulty catching his breath, but the doctor had as-sured him that he was getting better. It was just going to take time. He felt sure the doctor was right. The Great War was over, and he had survived. Now, a new life lay ahead with his beloved Doris and their child.

He reached over for Doris's hand and closed his eyes, thinking back on the past few days and his visit to his family.

The ride to the farm had seemed endless to Philip. Doris was so close to him, but his uncle's presence in the motorcar made any intimacy between the couple impossible. They made polite conversation, but anything of a personal nature would have to wait until they were alone. Philip couldn't take his eyes off Doris and thought her even more beautiful than he remembered.

When he wasn't looking at her, he looked aimlessly out the window, thinking how little the scenery had changed. Everything seemed to look pretty much as it did before he left for the war. When they finally pulled up to the farmhouse, his first thought was that, if anything, it looked worse than he remembered. The house was badly in need of painting, and he could see some loose shingles on the roof.

There was great excitement when Philip and Doris entered the house. His mother put her arms around him and held him close. Philip could see tears in her eyes as she said, "You're home at last. I had fears that I would never see you again."

Philip thought she looked older than her forty years. The losses she had suffered over the years, including the death of her baby, as well as the hard work on the farm, had taken their toll.

His stepfather Claude smiled briefly and shook his hand, saying, "Welcome home."

Philip saw his brother Charlie and said, "Wow, look how tall you are. I bet you've grown at least two inches since I last saw you."

Just a boy when Philip had joined the army, Charlie was now a grown man. He grinned as he stepped forward with a hearty handshake before Philip grasped his shoulders in a playful bear hug.

Nellie had held supper for them, and they sat down to eat and then lingered at the table, talking of Philip's recent trip home and catching up on news of the farm and various relatives and neighbors. After what seemed like forever, Philip and Doris ascended the stairs to Charlie's room, where they were to sleep, with Charlie following close behind, assisting with their belongings.

After Charlie took his leave, the two melted into each other's arms, kissing and laughing, so happy they were to once again be together. They began talking at the same time, rambling on excitedly about everything and nothing.

After a short time, Philip stopped talking and, looking closely at Doris, finally said, "Your hair! I've been trying to figure out what's different and just now realized it. You've cut your hair," he said as he stared at her chin length bob.

"You don't like it," she said.

Philip was quick to respond. "No, he said, "I mean, yes, I do like it very much. It looks very up-to-date, like pictures I saw in magazines at the camp library."

"Yes," said Doris. "It's the latest fashion. All my friends are cutting theirs, although our mothers are scandalized." She then smiled mischievously.

Although Philip had always admired Doris's long, wavy hair, he had to admit the style was becoming, and he felt a secret pride that she was a modern woman who wasn't stuck in the old ways like his mother and, he supposed, Doris's mother as well.

The time at the farm was uneventful. Philip felt somewhat restless but kept himself busy helping Claude and Charlie with the chores. Doris appeared to be at loose ends – not quite knowing what to do with herself. She offered to help Nellie with household tasks but, more often than not, received a polite refusal. Visits from nearby relatives and neighbors and a day trip to Battle Creek helped to fill some of the time. Evenings were spent in quiet conversation in the small sitting room, where Charlie would sometimes entertain them with his violin. The days ended early, as the work of the farm required early rising. Even in winter, there was a lot to do, and the days were long and tiring.

On their first night at the farm, Philip awoke in a cold sweat and felt unable to breathe. It was dark in the room, and at first, he wasn't sure where he was, but gradually became aware of someone sleeping beside him and realized that it was Doris. As his eyes adjusted to the darkness, he was able to identify the shapes of furniture and remembered he was back on the family farm. He and Doris had traveled there after his discharge and were spending a few days with his family. His brother Charlie had given up his bedroom and agreed to sleep downstairs on the sofa.

He felt the need to use the bathroom but wasn't sure he wanted to venture outside in the cold. The farm was now electrified but still didn't have an indoor toilet. Doris hadn't been happy about that. A city girl, she had never used an outdoor toilet. He could feel another fit of coughing about to overtake him, and, not wanting to wake Doris, he slipped quietly out of bed and walked out of the bedroom into the hallway and to the top of the stairs. He saw that there was a light on downstairs.

Someone must be up, he thought. *Probably Charlie.*

Charlie had always been a night owl who didn't seem to require much sleep. As Philip walked down the stairs, he could see Charlie sitting in the small parlor next to the only lamp in the room, smoking and reading a newspaper.

"It's late," Charlie said. "Couldn't you sleep?"

"I was having trouble breathing and was afraid I'd start coughing," Philip said. "I didn't want to wake Doris."

The exertion of walking downstairs and then talking caused Philip to start coughing forcefully.

Charlie stared at him, and when the coughing stopped, he asked, "Do you cough like that all the time?"

"Yes, I haven't really felt well since I left the hospital in France. The doctors say I am getting better, so I guess I just have to give it some time."

"What does Doris say about it?" Charlie asked.

"Not much," said Philip. "I try not to worry about her. I think I'll feel better once we get back to Syracuse and settle into a regular routine."

Philip sat and looked around the room. It was even shabbier than he remembered. He had been so eager to leave this place, but it was still home, and he was glad to see Charlie again. He lit a cigarette, and he and his brother sat quietly before Charlie broke the silence.

"What was it really like, being in the war?" he asked.

"It was horrible," Philip replied. "Worse than anything I could have imagined. When I enlisted in the army, I had dreams of seeing the world and becoming a hero, but I had a rude awakening. Seeing so many die and living every day in fear that it could happen to me, I wondered if I would make it home to see my wife and baby. I still have nightmares about being at the front. Sometimes, I wake up and don't know where I am – scared to death, I'm back there in the thick of it."

He talked to Charlie, telling him stories about the war, the battles he had been part of, and the things he had seen and done – stories he could never tell his wife or mother. At times, his eyes would fill with tears, but with great effort, he managed to control himself. Charlie asked an occasional question but mostly listened in silence. Philip remembered that Charlie had always been a good listener. They talked far into the night until the sky outside began to lighten, signaling the arrival of dawn.

For the remainder of the visit, Philip would head upstairs with Doris soon after Nellie and Claude retired. After Doris was asleep, he would return downstairs to the parlor, where he would join Charlie, and the two would sit and talk for the next couple of hours. They remembered good times and not-so-good ones, taking turns telling stories about the fun they had and the hard work they did.

"Remember the hiding places we had when Claude was looking for us to do extra work?" Charlie said with a grin.

"Yes," said Philip with a laugh, "And I remember the whippings we got when he sometimes found us."

They remembered the back-breaking work and the sparse meals they sometimes had when income from the farm was less than expected. They also remembered running through fields, climbing trees, and swimming in the pond on hot summer days.

They spoke of friends they had known and Philip wondered where they were. Charlie updated him about a few of them but wasn't sure about others.

Philip had never felt closer to Charlie and believed that no matter where their lives took them, the bond between them would always remain strong.

Doris shivered from the cold as she sat at the supper table. Outside, the weak winter sun was fading, and the temperature was dropping. When they first arrived at the farm, southern Michigan had been experiencing a spell of unseasonably warm weather, and they had been able to enjoy spending time outside. Philip had shown her around the small farm and they even walked down the road and visited his aunt and uncle.

The fine weather had continued the previous day, and Charlie had driven them to the nearby village of Marshall, where they caught a bus to Battle Creek. They had spent an enjoyable day walking around the small city, and Philip had shown her the Michigan Business and Normal College he had attended before joining the army, as well as the famous Kellogg's cereal plant. They had met up with a couple of his college friends and had a pleasant lunch at a small sandwich shop.

The day had been a welcome respite from spending time at the farm, where Philip's stepfather rarely spoke to her, and his mother, while cordial enough, could be seen casting disapproving glances her way when she thought Doris wasn't looking. Although Philip denied it, Doris was sure that the older woman didn't like her very much and probably didn't approve of her bobbed hair and shortened dresses (which, in fact, Doris's own mother didn't like either). Philip and Charlie spent a good part of the day helping with chores around the farm, so Doris was pretty much left on her own.

That morning, the weather had taken a bitter turn, becoming

much colder, with a biting wind that rattled the window panes and blew through the cracks of the old house. The wood stove and fireplace barely warmed the downstairs rooms, and the upstairs had no heat at all. Doris didn't even want to think about venturing out to use the outdoor privy and put it off as long as she could. The ground was now covered with an icy coating of snow, making the trek hazardous.

Although she was wearing her heaviest clothes, Doris was unable to get warm. Her feet were blocks of ice, and her hands and fingers were so cold and stiff that she had a hard time moving them. Living her whole life in upstate New York, she was well-acquainted with cold and snow, but she was used to a warm house. Her parents' home in Syracuse had a coal-fired boiler with ducts that carried heat to all parts of the house. *I'm glad that this is my last night here,* she thought.

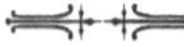

Philip sat at the table, looking around at the family members gathered there. Charlie had butchered one of their hens for the meal, much to his stepfather's annoyance. Philip had overheard an argument between his mother and her husband and had heard Claude protest loudly when Nellie told Charlie to kill the chicken.

Philip's mother, however, had been insistent, saying, "My son is home from the war, and I am going to make him a nice meal. I don't care what you say."

There had been a lengthy argument, but, in the end, his mother had won, and Charlie was sent to kill and pluck the feathers from the chicken – one of their older hens. Philip knew what a sacrifice that was as the hen was still a good layer, and the eggs they got from her provided food for the family or, if sold, added to the farm's meager income. Although Philip and his mother had often been at odds with each other, that evening, his heart was filled with love for her.

The hen was old, and although Nellie stewed it for a good part of the day, the meat remained somewhat tough and stringy. Regardless, Philip thought it tasted quite good, and the gravy was thick and rich. Nellie had never been an especially creative cook, but she had put great effort into preparing a fine meal, baking biscuits and adding vegetables from the root cellar to the stew pot. Philip's grandparents came for supper, and his grandmother brought a pie.

As he sat sharing the meal with his family, he felt the happiest he had felt in a long time and was glad to be there. *For better or worse, these people are my family, and I'll always love them.*

As much as he had enjoyed the visit, his return to the farm had reminded him of the reason he'd left and renewed his longing for a better life than could be had there. He was glad he and Doris would be leaving the next day. The time had come for them to finally start a new life together.

CHAPTER 20

Philip sat in the streetcar, making his way home. It was a bright, sunny day, and he felt a soft, warm breeze drifting in through the open window. It seemed that the long winter had finally broken, and spring had arrived. It was now late April, and leaves were beginning to pop out on trees, filling the air with a sweet scent as life once again renewed itself.

It was hard to believe that two years had passed since Philip left the army. So much had changed in the world and in the city of Syracuse. Women had been given the right to vote. The Volstead Act was passed, making it illegal to manufacture and sell alcoholic beverages. The Treaty at Versailles was signed, officially ending the Great War. That event was cause for celebration on July 4, 1919, at a large downtown parade.

The Erie Canal had been closed to navigation in 1917 and replaced by the Barge Canal, bypassing downtown Syracuse. Plans had begun filling in the canal, making way for paved streets, thereby bringing an end to one of the great engineering wonders of the nineteenth century. Boat traffic no longer traveled from "Albany to Buffalo" but rather up the barge canal to Lake Ontario and into the Great Lakes. Model Ts and other automobiles were now becoming the popular mode of transportation as more and more people were able to afford them.

Syracuse was experiencing great growth and development.

The salt industry had come to an end and manufacturing had taken its place as new companies continued to open and add to the workforce. Among the industries were soda ash, crucible steel, gears, traffic lights, and the Franklin Automobile. The city was also home to the typewriter industry and became known as the Typewriter City.

Philip was himself employed at the Smith Premier Typewriter Company, located in downtown Syracuse. With many men looking for employment after the war ended, Philip had been worried that he would be unable to find work. But, true to his word, his father-in-law, Horace Bowman, had assisted him in obtaining a position. Horace's mother-in-law, Jennie Bogardus, had a family connection with the Smith Premier Company, and Horace was able to put in a word for Philip.

Philip presently worked as a stockroom clerk, ordering and stocking parts for typewriters. He worked six days a week and hoped to move up to a better position. Philip worked hard but was often tired and sometimes slow, needing to take frequent rests. He hoped this wouldn't be noticed but had sometimes seen his boss looking at him.

Philip still had a bad cough, which had never gone away. He sometimes had a hard time catching his breath and would be overtaken by fits of coughing. The cough seemed to be worse at night, and lately, he had noticed blood when he coughed forcefully. He hadn't told Doris about this, not wanting to worry her. He had seen a doctor – referred by the Bowman's family physician – but he hadn't helped him much. The doctor had given him some cough syrup, which gave him some relief, especially at night, but made him groggy. He had been oversleeping lately and barely made it to work on time. Last week, he missed work entirely, unable to get out of bed. He had called his boss, explaining that he was ill. The excuse was accepted but he couldn't keep doing that. He didn't want to lose his job.

The drowsiness sometimes carried over through the day and

sometimes had a hard time staying awake. Philip was dozing in the car at present. The streetcar had come to a stop due to a number of motorcars, causing a jam. *It seems there are more and more cars every day,* he thought. His hope was to purchase one himself and was putting aside money to do that. His father-in-law had taught him to drive, and he liked the idea of driving rather than taking the streetcar to work. He also thought about how nice it would be to be able to take pleasurable drives with his family. As he sat in the streetcar in a dreamlike state, he thought about all his hopes and plans. There was so much he wanted to do and make a success in the world. After all, that was the whole idea of leaving the farm in hopes of a better life. He also wanted to give Doris the life she deserved. He loved her so much and would do anything to make her happy.

Doris sat in the parlor by herself, staring down at her feet. They were shod in a pair of plain brown oxfords – the ones she wore around the house. Doris was proud of her feet, which were tiny and perfectly formed. She had slim, shapely ankles, which Philip had remarked were one of the first things he'd noticed about her when she lifted her skirt to board a street car. Of course, that was when women wore longer dresses. After the war ended, hemlines started going up, and Doris, wanting to keep up with the latest fashions, shortened hers to mid-calf length, much to her mother's dismay.

Doris loved pretty clothes and had several nice dresses in the latest styles. She was a bright bird, and the pretty dresses were plumage that accentuated her lovely face. Her hair was fashionably bobbed, and she had an array of nice shoes to show off her pretty feet. She had spectator pumps and her favorite, shiny black dancing shoes with open toes and dainty straps. Doris loved to dance and thought of her feet as dancing feet. Her friend, Helen, had taught her the foxtrot, the two of them dancing around Helen's parlor to ragtime music played on the phonograph.

She was eager to go out dancing and try out the new steps at a local club she had heard about, but when she mentioned it to Philip, he said no, since he was too tired after working all day. He had changed since coming home from the war. He was quieter and not as much fun as he had been when they first met. She knew he didn't feel well. He was still feeling the effects of the gas attack he had suffered on the battlefield in France. He coughed a lot and, sometimes, had difficulty catching his breath.

At times, she wondered if she made a mistake in marrying in such haste. She was so taken by the handsome soldier and immediately fell head over heels in love with him. Then again, she had been so eager to escape the clutches of her parents. Longing to leave the nest, it all seemed so romantic and exciting, but things don't always turn out as expected. She immediately found herself pregnant. Then there was the long, lonely year still living with her parents. She missed having fun with her friends and going to parties. Still, she loved Philip and only wanted to have him back with her as she waited out the long year. She gave birth to her daughter and looked forward to the time she and Philip could begin their lives together.

When he returned, they were happy to be together again, and at first, things seemed to go well. They set up housekeeping in a small house not far from her parents, and Philip found a good job at a typewriter company. It wasn't long before she noticed that he had a bad cough that didn't seem to go away, even with the medicine the doctor gave him. He would come home from work exhausted and spend the evening sitting in the parlor. Lately, he had been missing time from work since he was unable to get out of bed in the morning. He sometimes woke in the middle of the night, unable to breathe. A couple of times, she had noticed blood when he coughed and had begun to wonder if he would ever get better. She truly loved Philip and worried about him, but wondered what would happen to her if he should die. She suspected she was pregnant again. Although she had pushed that thought from the back of her mind, not having yet mentioned it to Philip, the idea of being left a widow with two children was frightening to her, even though her parents wouldn't let them starve.

This wasn't the way she imagined her life would turn out. She sometimes felt jealous of her friend, Helen, who had gone to a business college and now had a good job at a downtown bank. She and a group of friends often went to parties in the evening and seemed to always be having fun. Helen even learned to drive a car and sometimes drove to see her in her father's Model T Ford.

In the meantime, her pretty dresses hung unworn in the closet, along with her shoes, and she spent her days doing mundane household chores and caring for her baby. She knew that others had it worse but still … She felt like a caged bird.

Philip got off at his stop and began making his way up St. Agnes Hill. The walk seemed to get longer every day. As he turned up the street, he brightened as he saw their little house in the distance. He looked forward to eating supper with Doris and playing with little Arnette, who was almost three years old. Doris was in the kitchen, and the food smelled good. Her mother taught her to cook and she had become quite a good cook. Doris had never been interested in cooking, but Philip thought the meals she made were very good. That night, she had made stew with meat, potatoes, and vegetables. It tasted quite delicious. Philip was easy to please, having never acquired a taste for rich or elaborate food. He was accustomed to plain food after growing up on the farm and then in the army.

After supper, Philip withdrew to the living room, sitting in his favorite chair. Arnette walked over and smiled up at him. She reached out to him, and he lifted her onto his lap. She hugged him, and his heart went out to her. He loved her so much, hardly believing she really belonged to him. As Arnette leaned against his chest, he put his arms around her and felt warmth and contentment flowing through him. Soon, both were asleep until they became aware of the light switching on in the room. Doris had finished her chores in the kitchen, and it was time for Arnette's bedtime.

Philip saw the newspaper sitting on a small table, delivered daily by a boy on a bicycle. He opened the paper and began to read until, after a time, Doris entered the room. They talked of Arnette and other happenings of the day.

Then, Doris said, "I got a telephone call from Mrs. Wise."

Philip had to think for a minute, "Oh, Andy's mother." It seemed so long since Andy died, although his memory had never left him. They made a sad visit to the Wises when they first returned to Syracuse but hadn't seen them since. "How is she doing?"

Doris said, "Well, as much as can be expected, I guess. One never gets over these things, but they still have their daughter, Mary, and they have a reason to keep going for her."

Philip said, "Yes, you're right."

"Well," Doris said, "Mary is now engaged to be married. They are planning a small party on Sunday, and she hopes we will come. Mary asked a few of Andy's friends. Mrs. Wise invited Helen Shore, and she plans to come as well."

Helen and Andy maintained a friendship after Philip and Doris were married. They were never romantically involved, but they liked each other very much. Helen had written to Andy during the war and, after he was killed, had written a condolence letter to Mrs. Wise. Since then, the two women kept in touch.

Doris then said, "It would be fun to see Helen. I haven't seen her for a while, and I always liked the Wises. We haven't been to a party in so long, and it would be fun to dress up a little and see some different people. I have already spoken to my mother, and she agreed to watch Arnette. "

Doris's eyes lit up and smiled brightly as she talked at length about the fun they would have at the party and how much she was looking forward to it.

Philip groaned inwardly. Sunday was his only day off, and he looked forward to resting and relaxing. He was just about to tell Doris to decline the invitation, but, seeing her happy expression, he acquiesced and said, "Yes, it would be nice to see the Wises as well as Helen."

Philip thought about the long streetcar ride out to Liverpool and back, and he started to feel tired already, but as Doris hugged him and saw her bright smile, it all seemed worth it to him.

CHAPTER 21

Philip felt tired already, although it was only Monday morning. He didn't know how he would manage to make it through the week until he had another day off. The party at the Wises' home lasted until the early evening, and by the time they drove home, it was time to go to bed. Before he knew it, it was time to get up for work.

Horace Bowman allowed them to use his motorcar, avoiding the long streetcar trip. If not for that, he would be even more tired and was grateful to his father-in-law. Doris had dressed up for the party, and he could see how much she was enjoying herself. As usual, she was the source of much male admiration. She always appreciated the attention and delighted in innocent flirting. Philip didn't really mind. As always, he was proud of her and knew she only belonged to him. Philip hadn't seen her look that happy in a while, and it probably caused him to stay much longer than he had planned.

He was glad to see the Wises as well as Helen Shore. He knew a few other people whom he had met through Andy – some they had known from Camp Syracuse. Most of the others were friends of Mary, and he didn't know them at all. He spent much of the time with those people, making polite conversation, and as the party dragged on, he just wanted to go home.

Philip felt weak and tired as he cranked up the motor of the

Model T and drove home. Doris talked happily all the way home. *Well, she deserved to have a little fun,* he thought; *she has little enough of it, although she rarely complains. She's a good wife and mother to Arnette.* He loved her so much and would do anything to make her happy.

Philip reached his stop and walked the short block and into the Smith Premier building. From the hallway, he could hear the clamor of metal parts being assembled and the voices of the men as they worked. He entered a large room that was filled with long rows of men as they worked to fashion the parts that would produce a typewriter. There was now a great demand for the typewriters, and it seemed they could not make them fast enough.

Philip walked through this room and into the stockroom which consisted of several shelves containing the parts that would be used for assembling the typewriters. His job was to keep track of the inventory as needed, order parts, and requisition them from the workers as they built the typewriters.

His friend, William Braun, was already working, busy unloading a box that had just come in and needed to be stocked on the shelves. Philip and Will had both started in the stockroom at the same time. A few years older than Philip, he was from the north side of Syracuse. A war veteran like himself, the two had become good friends. Unlike Philip, he wasn't married and lived at home with his parents. Will had his own car and often gave Philip a ride home from work. He was aware of Philip's breathing difficulties and could see that he struggled through the workday. He often took on the heavier tasks, leaving the lighter work for Philip.

Today, he said, "We had a big shipment come in. I'm going to unload these cartons. Why don't you work on the paperwork? I'm no good at that, and you're much better at it."

Philip sat at the desk and said, "There's a mountain of paper, some left from yesterday's shipment, but I'll get through it."

Philip was good at that aspect of the job, being especially adept at working with figures. He also appreciated the sedentary work as opposed to the job of lifting parts onto the higher shelves. Philip knew Will was doing him a favor and he greatly appreciated it. He was a good friend. Doris liked him as well, sometimes inviting him for supper.

Now Philip said, "Doris told me to ask you for supper tomorrow."

Will said, "Sure, I'd like that. I'll let my mother know not to expect me."

Will enjoyed spending the evening with Doris and their daughter Arnette. Although he hadn't yet met the right girl, he was hopeful he would eventually find one. He admired Doris and thought, wistfully, *If only I could meet someone like her.*

For her part, the admiration was not lost on her. She enjoyed his company and put special effort into preparing the food and spent time fixing her hair and applying lip color.

When it became time for their noon meal break, the two walked together to the lunch room. After the exertion of walking, Philip became overcome with coughing.

Finally, Will said, "Have you seen a doctor about your coughing?"

Philip said, "Of course, I saw several doctors in the Army, and they just seemed to say it might take a while for the effects of the gas attack to go away, but I guess I didn't think it was going to be this long. I did see the Bowmans' doctor, but he didn't say much, and the medicine he gave me didn't seem to help much. It makes me too sleepy."

"I recently heard about a good doctor," Will said. "He's a young doctor and is a veteran himself. He's up on all the latest methods and medicines. I can find out his name if you want."

Philip said, "Yes, I have to do something. I have felt ill since I came home from the war. I can't go on like this. Yes, please give me his name."

Will said, "I don't know his telephone number, but I can find out for you. I do know he has an office downtown, not far from here. I'll find out the information for you."

It took Will some time l to get back to Philip with the information, and it took more time for Philip to make the appointment. Philip needed a late afternoon or evening visit that wouldn't interfere with his job. Spring had become summer as Philip sat in the office of Dr. Benjamin Green on a hot, humid late afternoon. The two spent time talking, and then Dr. Green carefully examined him. Philip was taken to another room where his lungs were X-rayed and a blood sample was taken.

As Dr. Green thoughtfully reviewed the information, Philip said, "Well, what do you think, Doctor?"

Dr. Green said, "We have to wait until all the results come back from your tests, but I'm quite sure that you have tuberculosis."

Philip sat in stunned silence. His mouth felt dry, and he felt cold. *Could it really be true?* he thought. Of course, he knew about tuberculosis; there were reports in the newspapers, and it had become a serious problem, but he never considered it for himself. He never even knew anyone who had it.

Philip said, "Could it just be caused by the gas attack?"

Dr. Green said, "Well, I'm sure that would enter into it, having weakened your lungs, but we can't rule it out. You spent many months in Europe, where tuberculosis is rampant, and among service men spent in close quarters. Why don't you make an appointment for next week? By then, the tests will be back, and we can go from there."

Philip's thoughts were in a whirl as he rode home on the street car. *It can't be true that I have tuberculosis. But maybe Dr. Green seemed to think it was very possible. Then what will I do? Will I get better? I don't know. What about Doris? How can I tell her?*

When Philip arrived at his house, Doris was at the door.

"What did the doctor say?" she said.

"Well," Philip said, "he's not sure yet, but he thinks I may have tuberculosis. I'll go back in a week when he'll know for sure."

The color drained from her face, and she stared at him. Then she began to cry. The two wrapped their arms around each other, not saying anything. There were no words to say. As they looked down, they saw that Arnette was looking up at them with a puzzled expression.

At last, Doris said, "I guess it's time to eat," and Doris helped Arnette into her chair. She had now graduated from her high chair and was able to sit on a cushion at the table.

The three sat together, but Philip and Doris had little appetite and only picked at their food. Later that night, Philip lay in the dark. He could hear Doris quietly crying, and he reached over to comfort her.

As Philip waited to keep his appointment with the doctor, he held on to a thread of hope that he would have good news, that he didn't have tuberculosis after all; there was some other condition that could easily be treated.

Finally, he found himself once again in Dr. Green's office. As he sat across from the doctor and after offering a few pleasantries, Dr. Green got straight to the point.

"I'm afraid there is no way to make this any better," Dr. Green said. "You have tuberculosis. The X-rays and tests have confirmed that."

Philip stared at him. "What happens now?" he said. "Is there a medicine you can give me that will cure it?"

Dr. Green sadly shook his head, "I'm sorry to say there is no medicine at present that will cure it. There are medicines that have been used in the past, but those have been discredited and are no longer used. Scientists around the world continue to find a cure, but currently, the answer hasn't been found."

"Do you mean," Philip said, "that nothing can be done?"

"No, that's not entirely true," Dr. Green said. "There are some things we can do. It's been found that a regimen of complete rest, a nutritious diet, and plenty of fresh air could alleviate symptoms. Living at a high altitude can also be beneficial. The sanatorium movement started in Europe, in the mountains of places like the Swiss Alps. Later, sanatoriums began opening in this country. One of the first was here in New York State – the Trudeau Institute at Saranac Lake. Of course, those places are far away, and there is a long waiting list for the number of patients that can be cared for."

Philip stared blankly into space, not quite knowing what to say, his thoughts in a whirl.

Dr. Green then said, "We do have some other choices that can be made. One of the best sanatoriums can be found here in this area, in Oswego County at Orwell, started by Dr. Hollis. I have visited the facility and was very impressed with the care there. It's located at a high elevation, far from urban areas where the air is fresh and clean. My second choice is the Onondaga County Sanitorium, here in Syracuse, on Onondaga Hill. In either case, they have long waiting lists, but I'll put you on the list for both.

In the meantime, you must immediately stop working. I'll call your employer today. I will also send a report to the Onondaga County Public Health Authority. You'll be visited by the public health nurse to assist you with your care while you're at home. You'll need to sleep in a room by yourself. The window needs to be open, no matter what the weather. Bed rest is imperative. You need to rest, but on nice days, you can sit outside or take short walks for exercise. Eat plenty of good, nutritious food."

Philip said, "How can I do all that? I can't just quit my job. I have a family to support. How in the world can I pay for care in a hospital?"

Dr. Green said, "You're a disabled veteran and are entitled to compensation as well as hospital care. I'll do the paperwork. You needn't worry about that."

But Philip did worry about it. The long, lonely trip home was filled with anxiety and outright fear.

CHAPTER 22

Philip watched as a bumble bee flew in and out of the flowers in the small garden. He saw a robin pecking in the grass and then pulled a worm from the ground. As the bird flew off, two squirrels chased each other through the yard and then scampered up a nearby tree.

Philip watched from the small porch of his house. It was a pleasant early September day. Although the calendar warned that fall was approaching, it seemed that summer was lingering later than usual, and the weather continued to be warm. The last few days had brought intermittent rain showers, but today was a bright sunny day.

Philip was now confined mostly to his bedroom. Horace Bowman and Will Braun had helped move another bed into Arnette's bedroom, where Doris now slept. Philip still awaited a bed in the sanatorium as soon as it became available. In the meantime, he was visited weekly by a county public health nurse. The nurse examined him and gave instructions to Doris about his care. Doris was given a cloth mask to wear whenever she entered the room. Others were forbidden entry. Arnette was only able to talk to him from the door of the room. Philip knew that Arnette didn't really understand why he wasn't allowed to hug her or sit on his lap, and his heart broke for her. He missed her terribly. Doris was now due to deliver a new baby in late October. He worried about her when he was finally admitted into the sanitorium – left on her own with two young children. Of course, he could depend on the Bowmans to help her, and he had also received his compensation money from the government, so he knew his family would be cared for.

Philip was allowed to exercise, and that morning, he had taken a short walk in the neighborhood. He was actually feeling a little better since he stopped working. The early morning rising, along with the streetcar ride and the long days working in a stuffy office, had all taken their toll. He now spent his days resting with the windows wide open. He made sure he had plenty of good food – meat, fruit, and vegetables, and drank fresh, clean water. He sometimes wondered if he really needed to go to the sanatorium. He thought, *Maybe I will get over it by myself.* He was told, however, after making a recent visit to the doctor, that his X-ray continued to show that he still had a spot on his lung, and he was told to keep to the original plan to enter the sanatorium whenever a bed was available.

Today, as he sat on the porch, he enjoyed the world around him and the sights and sounds of nature. He continued to believe he would get better – it was just going to take time.

Doris came out on the porch and sat heavily in the other rocking chair on the porch. As he looked at her, she appeared tired. They expected their second baby sometime next month. He continued to be amazed by the difference as she changed from the slim girl he had once known. Of course, he hadn't seen her during her first pregnancy, so this was all new to him. In any case, none of this mattered to him. He thought her still as beautiful as always.

Doris now looked into the yard and said, "Will is going to come by today and mow the lawn."

Philip said, "He's such a good friend."

Will often stopped by on his day off and helped around the house, doing repairs that sometimes needed to be made now that Philip wasn't able to do them.

Doris said, "Yes, we don't know what we'd do without him."

Doris then drew two letters from her apron pocket. She said, "One is from your mother, and the other was delivered to my parents. I think it may be from one of your Army buddies,"

Philip looked at the return address and saw "Joe Kowalski, Toledo, Ohio."

"Joe Kowalski," Philip said in amazement. "I haven't thought about Joe in so long. We exchanged addresses just before one of our big battles, hoping to keep in touch in case we were separated, but I lost track of mine after I was gassed and then sent to the hospital. I wondered what had happened to him."

The two talked for a time, and then Doris returned to the house. Philip opened his letter from Joe.

September 5, 1921

Dear Phil,

I found my old Army pack, and as I went through it, there was the address you had given me in care of your father-in-law, Horace Bowman. I suppose you are now living somewhere else, but hopefully, the letter will find its way to you. I imagine you have found a job there in Syracuse and are happy to be back with your wife and daughter.

We heard you had been gassed and sent to a hospital far away but never heard anything after that. There was great confusion after that final battle, and then the war ended. We stayed in France for a few months. We marched into Coblenz Bridgehead and stayed there as part of the occupation. We had the usual duties but had some time to do a little traveling.

We finally got our orders and left France in August 1919. When I got home, I went to see Anne and told her I wanted to marry her no matter what. We went to my priest but were told that we couldn't be married in the church unless Anne were to give up her own faith and become a Catholic. Of course, she didn't want to do that, as her parents were very upset by it. Also, my parents were determined that we be properly married in the church. My grandparents are from the old country and have strong beliefs about those things.

We finally went to Anne's minister, who agreed to marry us. We had a small wedding, just Anne's parents and a few friends. My parents refused to come, and things weren't good with them for a while, but things changed after we had our son, Joseph III. We brought him over to see them, and of course, they loved him. Things are better now. They love Anne, and I'm working in my father's store. We are expanding our business, and things are going great.

I wanted to let you know how things turned out. You always told me not to give up, and that turned out to be true. I hope that will be the same for you. Please write back and give me your news and how things are going with you.

Your friend,
Joe Kowalski

Well, I'm glad things turned out okay for Joe. I'll have to write to him. It will be hard to tell him about learning I have tuberculosis and going into the sanatorium. Well, I'll get around to finding a way to tell him.

The second was from his mother. He had finally told her about his illness and his imminent admission to the sanatorium.

September 7, 1921

Dear Philip,
I have read your letter and am sorry to hear about your illness. I hope you will get better in the hospital. I hope your wife and baby Arnette are well. I know you told me that Doris will be expecting a new baby and hope to hear about that news when it happens.

Charlie was quite distressed about your illness. He was all set to get on a train to see you, but I discouraged him from leaving. He is needed here on the farm. We can't do without him. We are both getting older and things aren't going as well as they could be. The recent crops haven't been as good as expected, and we are holding on for dear life. We don't want to lose the farm.

I haven't told you yet, but we are now expecting another baby ourselves. The baby will be due sometime in November, and I hope to give birth and have a healthy baby.

I'll wait to hear more from you and please send me your new address in the sanatorium so I can write to you.

With love,
Mother

So he will now have a new baby sister, he thought, *well, I guess they are probably happy. I hope things go better for them this time.* He well remembered Glen, who had died when he was only a few months old after a bout of diphtheria, not long before he entered the Army.

Philip didn't know they were experiencing such dire straits regarding the farm. No one had mentioned it to him. *I'll have to write to Charlie about it, although there won't be much I can do to help them. Charlie will do whatever he can to help them, but I'm sorry to have the entire thing falling on him. He deserves to have a life of his own, maybe meet a nice girl.*

He heard a car and saw Will Braun drive up in his car. He waved and said hello to Philip and then headed toward the small shed behind the house. Before long, he began mowing the lawn. Philip knew he appreciated it, and Doris was grateful for it as well. It would be too difficult for her to do it, and while Horace Bowman was good about helping out with these tasks, the Bowmans were already helping a lot. Will didn't seem to mind helping out. Doris would undoubtedly have invited him to supper, and she would enjoy the company. As usual, he would eat alone at a small table in his room.

A short time after that, Philip received a letter from the Onondaga County Health Department informing him of his admission to the sanatorium. Within a few days, he packed his personal belongings and was driven by his father-in-law to the facility, where he became the ninth World War veteran to be admitted to the sanatorium. He had not yet reached his 24th birthday.

CHAPTER 23

November 15, 1921

Dear Philip,

I miss you. It's now getting colder, as you know. I'm still recovering from Beverly's birth but getting up for short periods and for meals. My mother comes every day and spends most of the day caring for the girls. She doesn't seem to mind.

My father calls the sanatorium often and gets reports about how you are doing. He is always told that you are doing as well as expected. We've been told that visitors are not allowed at the sanatorium. I hope and pray that you will get better soon.

Our baby, Beverly Janice, is very beautiful. She has bright blue eyes like Arnette, but the two girls don't really look like each other. My mother seems to feel she favors me, whereas Arnette looks more like you. She's a good baby and seems to be healthy. My mother has talked about having a photographer come in and take her picture so you can see what she looks like. It's hard to believe that another baby is here, and once again, you're not here to see her.

I love you and miss you. I am sending kisses to you and from your daughters.

Love,
Doris

Horace Bowman had called the sanatorium with news of the new baby girl. The word spread among the sufferers on the ward, bringing about an element of excitement and a momentary bright spot in an otherwise drab day.

Philip and Doris had decided on a name for their baby. Doris had difficulty finding a boy's name, feeling Horace was "perfectly awful" and just couldn't give a baby such a name. She also didn't like Philip's father's name, Sherman. They had finally decided on Charles as a boy. Doris decided on Beverly after reading a popular novel about the heroine of the same name. Doris thought the name romantic, and Philip thought it pleasant enough. Doris chose Janice, a popular name at the time, for a middle name.

Philip had settled in at the sanatorium. He sometimes felt as though he were back in the army hospital, seeing the ward filled with long rows of beds occupied with men in various stages of tuberculosis. He had met some of them, and like himself, some were veterans of the World War.

The mail had come earlier in the day, but the letter from Philip continued to sit unopened on the table.

Louise entered the room and said, "Why, Doris, you haven't opened your letter from Phillip. Don't you want to know what he has to say?"

Doris looked at the letter without much interest but finally opened it and began to read.

December 10, 1921

Dear Doris,
I hope this letter finds you well. I miss you and both my sweet girls.

My days are going along well. It's getting colder, but they still want us to get out each day as long as there is no rain or snow. We walk out on the trails among the trees around the buildings. We are to take deep breaths in order to get plenty of fresh air into our lungs.

I see a physical therapist twice a week. They also have an occupational therapist but was told I didn't need that. I'm able to dress and tie my shoes, as well as be able to eat by myself. The physical therapist takes me into a room with various equipment, and I work out with him, hoping to build up my strength.

I am now designated as an "up patient," which means I'm able to be up at times during the day. I still spend most of the day resting in bed but am able to go to the dining room for meals. The food is pretty good. They told me the food comes from the county farm.

We sleep with the windows open, whatever the weather. Thank you for sending the warm sweater and blankets. I'm sure it's going to get even colder as the winter progresses.

Please give kisses and hugs to you and our girls.

Love,
Philip

Doris finished reading the letter and then returned it to its envelope. She heard a soft cry from Beverly as Louise brought the baby to Doris for her feeding. After she finished, she sat looking at Beverly. She decided that she did look different from Arnette. Her hair was darker, and Arnette's lighter brown was more like Philip's. As she sat looking at her baby, she suddenly felt an overwhelming sadness and felt tears begin to fall down her cheeks. She saw her mother coming into the room and quickly wiped them away.

Louise picked up the baby and said to Doris, "It's time for you to get dressed. It's almost noon."

Doris would spend most of the day in her night clothes if given the chance. After dressing, Doris returned to the chair in the living room and sat staring into space. There was a small stack of three or four books that Louise had picked up for her from the library. Doris had always enjoyed reading, especially romance novels.

Louise said, "The librarian especially recommended these, and I think you'll like them."

Doris now looked at them without interest. Like most other things, she didn't seem to have much interest in anything.

Louise said, "Helen has called several times, but she said you haven't answered her calls. She'd like to visit you. She hasn't yet seen Beverly."

Doris said, "I'll call her."

"Well," Louise said, "She's coming tomorrow. She'll be here at two o'clock. It will be good for you to have some company."

Doris sighed, "Yes, it'll be good to see her."

Helen arrived the next day as promised. The two visited and spent time catching up on their news. Helen fussed over the baby.

"She's so beautiful," she said, "She looks like you."

Doris admired the pink sweater and hat that Helen's mother had made.

The girls visited, and the afternoon lingered on. Louise brought out some cookies along with a pot of tea. Helen talked about her job at the bank and then talked about other friends they knew.

Finally, it was time for Helen to leave. The girls hugged, and then they said their goodbyes, promising to see each other soon, but after Helen left, she felt tears begin to sting her eyes.

Louise said, "It was so nice to see Helen again."

Doris nodded. She suddenly felt tired. "I think I'll take a nap," she said.

Philip received the following from his mother.

December 20, 1921

Dear Philip,
Your new baby sister arrived on November 30. We have named her Agnes Lucille, and we are so happy with her. I'm still not up and around yet, but your cousins are good about coming around most days and assisting with the baby and helping with housework and meals. Of course, I'm not able to do that, but thankfully, it is wintertime, and there isn't as much to do. Charlie is good about doing what needs to be done.

I'm tired, so I will end this. I hope you are getting better. We all think of you often. I hope Doris and the two girls are doing well.

Love,
Mother

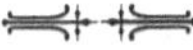

Philip wrote:
January 5, 1922

Dear Charlie,
I heard from Mother with the news about the new baby girl, Agnes Lucille. She didn't mention anything about the farm and wondered whether things have improved. She wrote to me in the fall and said they were hanging on for dear life. I'm not sure what to think about that.

I'm sure you now know about our new daughter, Beverly Janice. I haven't seen her yet. They are not allowed in the sanatorium. They said when the weather is warm, they can sit outside and visit me there. I guess that won't be for a while. It's very cold and snowy here. We still sleep with the windows wide open. They pile many blankets on my bed each night.

I'm able to get up at times during the day, and I'm able to read, write letters, and get up for meals. I've met some of the men. There's a recreation room, and we sometimes play cards or board games.

I miss all of you and hope things are going well on the farm. Hope to hear from you soon.

Your brother,
Phil

Charlie responded:
January 30, 1922

Dear Phil,
Things here on the farm are about the same. As I told you, we had a poor crop as well as some expensive repairs that needed to be done. We finally scraped up enough for our winter supplies and the spring seeds but needed to take out a mortgage on the farm. It was either that or sell a couple of our cows and we didn't want to do that, so we decided on the mortgage. If we have a good crop this year and sell a lot at the market, things will go well, and we can pay off the mortgage.

Please don't worry about it. Something will work out. I hope you are getting better. We all think of you often.

Your brother,
Charlie

Doris sat at the window looking out at the snow. She rarely ventured outside these days. It was too cold, and it seemed there was no reason to go. She did what was needed for the care of her baby, but otherwise, she had little interest in anything else. Her mother continued to come daily and spend part of the day. She felt that Louise hovered over her and wished she would just leave her alone.

As Doris looked out the window, she saw William Braun pull into the driveway.

I haven't seen Will in so long, she thought. She rarely had any company these days and smiled at the thought of seeing him.

Will was no longer working at Smith Premier and had completed his exam to become a firefighter for the City of Syracuse. He still kept in touch with Philip through letters, and he had stopped to see her soon after Philip went into the sanatorium. As always, he offered to do anything she might need, but most of his time was now occupied with his fire training. He had completed his training but worked irregular shifts at the firehouse.

As Doris saw him pull in, she realized she hadn't even combed her hair that day. She went into the bedroom, quickly straightened her hair, and applied a little color to her lips and cheeks. She heard Louise answer the door, and after speaking for a few minutes, Doris heard the door close and watched him drive off.

Doris said, "Wasn't that Will Braun I heard at the door?"

"Yes," Louise said, "He stopped by to see if you needed some help. He has a day off, but I told him your father is able to do anything that needs to be done, and if he needs help, Uncle Eugene can help."

Doris said, "Will likes to help; he's our good friend, and I would have liked to have seen him. Why couldn't he have just come in and said hello."

Louise said, "It really isn't appropriate to be entertaining men while your husband is away."

Doris had a hard time holding in her temper. *She still wants to control me. I'm a married woman, and I can make my own decisions.* Her eyes filled with tears and turned away, retreating to the bedroom and closing the door.

Nothing more was said about Will, but Doris decided to call him herself. On the day that Louise was out of the house, she found Will's telephone number and placed a call to his mother.

"Hello, Mrs. Braun," Doris said, "My name is Mrs. Philip Boughton – my husband is a friend of your son, William."

Mrs. Braun said, "Oh, yes, of course, I've heard William speak about Philip. How is your husband doing? I know he's in the hospital."

Doris said, "He seems to be doing as well as can be expected. I have a message from him to your son. I know that he now lives at the firehouse, but I'm hoping that you have a number where I can reach him."

Mrs. Braun said, "You're right. William spends most of his time at the firehouse, but he does come home on his days off. I expect him later this week, and I'll tell him you are trying to reach him. Should I take your number, or does he already have it?"

Doris said, "Yes, he does have the number, and I would appreciate a call from him."

Doris made sure to answer the telephone whenever it rang. Will called within a few days and sounded pleased to hear from her.

Will said, "I stopped at your house recently but was told by your mother that you don't need any help. I got the feeling that she would prefer that I not have any contact with you."

Doris said, "Oh, don't pay any attention to her. She likes to tell me what to do. I can decide for myself who I want to see. I'd like to see you. You've helped us so much, and I know Philip appreciates it too."

Will said, "I'd really like to see you and the girls and hear the news about Phil. I don't have another day off this week, but I can come early next week."

Doris said, "That would be good, and if I know you are coming, I'll watch for you and let you in."

"Okay," he said, "I'll let you know what time I'll be there."

Will came as promised. Louise had already been there and gone home to start her own supper and take care of some chores. When she stopped to see Doris later, she wasn't happy to see Will's car in the driveway. The two were engaged in conversation when she entered the room and spoke to Will with a terse greeting but said nothing more.

Will admired the new baby and spent time talking with Arnette. The child missed her father very much and didn't often have an opportunity to interact with a young man like Will. She enjoyed the attention, and Doris felt grateful as she saw Arnette's beaming smile. Will talked about his new job as a firefighter and asked about Philip and his condition. Will was disappointed that he was not able to visit him.

Doris said, "We've been told that we can visit him when the weather gets better, and we'll be able to sit outside and visit him there."

Doris offered to make tea or coffee, but Will said, "No, I really can't stay too long. My mother has some things she wants me to do. I can stop again if you want the next time I have a day off. Please let me know if there is anything I can do."

Doris spoke of some things she needed to do, and Will agreed to help her.

After Will left, Louise said, "I don't feel it is appropriate to entertain another man in the house."

She started to elaborate, but Doris held up her hand to stop her. "Please, Mother, don't say, 'What will the neighbors say?' I can make my own decisions, and I'm not doing anything inappropriate. Will is a good friend to me and to Philip, and I enjoy his company. So, please stop telling me what to do."

Doris then said, "Will has offered to take me downtown to Dey Brothers Department Store, where I've heard they now carry a large assortment of home goods. I still have the curtains that are hanging in the sitting room that Grandmother Jennie gave us when we first moved in. I've never liked them, and they make the room dark and drab. I'd like to pick out new ones. Will has even offered to hang them for me. It would brighten up the room."

Doris couldn't remember the last time she had been downtown, and she was eager to see the newly improved department store.

She then said, "Yes, I know Dad can do it, but he has enough to do, and Will is happy to help."

Doris also knew that her father wouldn't want to spend much time there, and she wanted to look around and take her time. Horace wouldn't have much patience for that. Will also suggested (although she neglected to mention this to Louise) that he would treat her to lunch at a cafeteria downtown, and she was looking forward to the outing.

Louise knew there was no changing Doris's mind. It also occurred to her that Doris's former spirit was returning, and she was glad to see that she was taking an interest in her home after not having much interest in anything. Well, she would keep an eye on things, but Doris was a good girl at heart and she did love Philip and her girls.

Doris calmed down and realized that her mother was only acting in her best interest. Doris also knew that as much as she liked Will, her heart only belonged to Philip. She was aware that Will secretly admired her and she did like the attention, but she also knew that he would never do anything to hurt Philip or come between them. She decided to write a letter to Philip tonight and tell him about the meeting with Will and their plans for the shopping outing.

CHAPTER 24

Doris wrote:
March 1, 1922

Dear Philip,

I got a surprise visit from Will Braun today. As you know, he is now a firefighter and lives at the firehouse. He's eager to tell you all about it and hear how you are faring in the sanatorium. He would like to visit you, but I told him you aren't allowed to have visitors. We made plans to see you when the weather improves enough to visit you outside.

We had a nice visit and Will very much wants to do anything he can to help us. He has promised to take me downtown to Dey Brothers Department Store where I want to buy some new curtains for the sitting room. As you know, the curtains are in sad condition, and new ones will greatly brighten up the room. Will has even offered to hang the new ones for me!

The girls are doing well. Arnette misses you very much. I read her your last letter. She listened and was very interested. She asked several questions and seems to be very smart. As you know, she'll be four years old in a few months and she is getting tall and growing out of her clothes, needing the hems let down. When the weather gets better, I'll take her downtown on the streetcar and pick out some new clothes.

With love and kisses from your wife and daughters,
Doris

P hilip frowned as he read the letter. He hoped Doris wasn't taking advantage of Will, toting her around, carrying out frivolous errands. He probably had better things to do with his time but may have had a hard time saying no. Philip can't recall that the curtains had looked that bad, but if so, her father could have taken her.

Well, she seems to have made up her mind and there would be no changing It.

March 15, 1922

Dear Doris,
I was glad to hear the news about Will. I also got a letter from him not long after you wrote. He told me all about the fire training. I wish I could see him again. We always had such good talks together. He reminds me a lot of Andy Wise. He was always ready to help, and I know I can depend on Will, too.

I'm glad you are now reading my letters to Arnette. I think I'll write her a letter of her own. I'll do that soon. Please let her know that she can expect a letter from me.

Love from your husband,
Philip

Doris watched as Will finished putting up the new curtains in the sitting room. As he hung them in the last of the two windows, he turned and looked around for her approval. That confirmation was all he needed as he saw her wide smile.

"Oh," she said, "Look how beautiful they are and how much brighter the room is. Mother, Arnette, come and look."

As the two entered from the kitchen, both smiled, and Arnette clapped her hands. Louise said, "They look beautiful! You were right to get them. They make a big difference."

Louise had felt the curtains were a frivolous expense but she had to agree they made the room much more cheerful.

Two weeks ago, Louise had minded the girls while Doris and Will made the trip to the downtown department store. They entered the store and rode the elevator, going from floor to floor, looking at everything. When they found the home furnishings department, Doris approached the counter.

The saleslady said, "May I help you?"

Doris opened her purse and carefully unfolded the page she had torn from *The Ladies Home Journal.*

The saleslady looked at the page and smiled, "Oh yes, white lace curtains are very popular now. We have a large selection, and they are on sale today."

Doris selected two pairs of curtains, and after paying for them, they left the store. It was a mild day and they walked along Salina Street, looking in the store windows. Doris admired the latest fashions at E.W. Edwards, L.A. Witherall, and C.E. Chappells and Sons. They ate lunch at a cafeteria and Doris enjoyed a bowl of vegetable soup with a slice of chocolate cake..

Doris said goodbye to Will at the door, and then she showed Louise the curtains. They were too long, but Louise promised to help her shorten them. Now Louise admired the curtains, and while she hadn't entirely approved of the expedition, she had to admit she hadn't seen Doris that happy in a long time.

Doris looked at the white lace curtains with their embossed designs and delicately scalloped edges. The windows had shades that could be lowered at night but were now raised to let in the light. It was a bright, sunny day, and the curtains shone through the windows. Doris thought about the many hours she had sat and looked at the old curtains with their dark colors and the large, old-fashioned floral pattern. There were many things she could not change in her life, but this was something she could.

Well, she said, *I won't have to look at them anymore.*

Philip received a letter from Charlie.

April 15, 1922

Dear Phil,
It has been raining here for days, and our field is now underwater. I don't seem to remember such a rainy spring. We are unable to plant our seeds, and I fear all our crops will be late. If we don't have a good enough crop, we may not be able to pay off the mortgage.

Our new sister Agnes is now over four months old. She's a quiet baby, and Mother and Claude are happy with her. Mother seems to be feeling better. She's up and around and taking care of the baby. Everyone is irritable with the constant rain. We think about you. I didn't think you would have to stay this long. Are you getting better? I keep thinking about a trip to see you, but right now, I'm needed here on the farm.

Your brother,
Charlie

Philip didn't know what to think about these reports from Charlie. There had been bad weather in the past and they always seemed to get through them. From what Charlie said, things seemed especially desperate. *Are they in danger of losing the farm?*

Philip didn't want to have to worry about the Osborns. He had enough worries of his own. He had his wife and daughters to think about and, of course, his own health.

As the winter wore on, Philip wondered if it would ever end. He continued to sleep with the windows wide open. Sometimes, he woke to find his blanket covered with a dusting of snow, having drifted in from the blowing wind.

At last, the weather started to show signs of spring. The snow melted, only to return again, but it didn't last long. There were more sunny, warm days and leaves started to pop out on the trees. The grass began to turn bright green and Philip noticed a robin on a branch outside his window. On days the weather was fair, he was now once again allowed outdoors in the fresh air.

Alone with his thoughts as he walked the trails, he realized that he had been in the sanatorium for over six months; *I never thought it would be that long.* He wondered how long it took to cure tuberculosis. He didn't recall any of the men on his ward being discharged to home. He had regular visits with the doctor, and occasional X-rays were taken, but he was never told anything.

I'm going to speak to the doctor about it the next time I see him. But, like always, he was given a vague answer. *I wonder if they really know when I'll get better,* he thought. *Maybe they don't really know.*

Philip watched as each car drove up the road and turned into the sanatorium parking lot.

"No," he said, "It's not them."

He held his hand above his eyes to shield them from the sun, and with each car, he again said, "No, I don't see them."

The nurse standing next to him smiled and said, "They'll be here."

Philip sat in a wooden Adirondack chair on the lawn near the sanatorium building.

Today was a warm, sunny day, and he was finally going to see Doris and their daughters. Although he had seen pictures of Beverly, he had not yet met her. Doris had made an appointment to visit him outside, and Will Braun had agreed to drive them. At last, he recognized Will's car and saw them walking along the path. Doris was carrying little Beverly as Arnette skipped along beside her. Will was carrying a blanket. As they approached, they stopped and waited for the instructions from the nurse. The nurse pointed and Will spread the blanket nearby.

The nurse said, "You can't get any closer. Mr Boughton is still contagious," and to Arnette, she said, "I know you want to hug your daddy, but you will need to stay on the blanket."

Arnette gravely nodded and then smiled at Philip, saying, "Hi, Daddy. I miss you,"

Philip had a hard time holding back tears. "I miss you too. You have gotten so tall."

"Yes," Doris said, "She is outgrowing her clothes. All her hems need letting down. Next week, we're going to take the streetcar downtown and meet Helen. We're going to one of the department stores to take a ride in the elevator and pick out a new dress for her. After we finish our shopping, we will go to Schrafft's for lunch. If she's a good girl, Helen has promised to treat her to a dish of strawberry ice cream."

Philip looked at Beverly, who was now able to sit by herself. "She looks just like you," he said.

Philip talked to Doris and Arnette and then asked a few questions of Will about what it was like to work at the firehouse. Will asked about his treatment and whether he thought he was getting better.

Philip said, "Yes, I think I am. It's now been over six months, and surely I should start seeing some improvement. I'm going to ask one of the doctors and have an X-ray. I have hopes that I'll soon be home."

Doris listened to this exchange and smiled as if in agreement, but she felt doubtful. Philip didn't look good to her. He appeared pale and seemed thinner.

She thought to herself, *I know he gets good food; why is he losing weight?*

She said nothing, but she couldn't help worrying.

Soon, the nurse told them it was time to leave. "You can come again, but the visits have to be short so as not to tire him."

Philip watched them go. As sad as he was to see them leave, the visit had exhausted him, and he was ready for some rest.

CHAPTER 25

Philip got back to his room just as the maid had finished making his bed, and he was happy to climb into it. The visit with his family had taken its toll, both physically and emotionally. He had wanted to see his wife and daughters so badly but hadn't realized it would be so hard to see them from a distance and to watch them leave. He wondered when he would see them again. As he looked at the girls, he could see they were growing up.

I'm missing so much of their lives. Why, Beverly doesn't even know who I am!

The nurse came over to his bed to take his temperature, and he asked her, "I want to make an appointment to see the doctor."

She said, "Is there a problem?"

He said, "Well, no, I just have something I need to talk to him about."

She said she would arrange an appointment the next time the doctor is available. A few days later, Philip was taken into a treatment room.

When he saw the doctor, he said, "I've been here for almost eight months now, and I still haven't been given a time when I can go home. It seems that I should be getting better by this time. I'd like another X-ray to see if there is any improvement in my condition."

The doctor looked at his chart and said, "Well, Mr Boughton, you had a recent X-ray, and there was no change."

Philip said, "Could you please try another one? I've been trying to walk more and get out in the fresh air, taking deep breaths. I think that's helping."

The doctor weighed him and gave him a thorough examination. He then listened carefully to Philip's chest and again reviewed the chart.

He appeared dubious, but after seeing the pleading look in Philip's eyes, he said, "I guess we can try another one."

Two views of Philip's chest were taken, and the doctor said, "I'll let you know after they have been developed."

Philip was told a few days later that there hadn't been any further improvement.

The doctor told him that, "It's good that it hasn't spread to the other lung. Continue to get as much fresh air into your lungs and try to eat better. You've lost some weight."

Philip tried to get out as the weather warmed but found he could only walk a short distance before becoming breathless. He tried to eat more but found he had little appetite.

Over the summer, Doris and Arnette, and sometimes Beverly, made occasional visits. Twice they were driven by Horace Bowman and once Doris and Arnette crossed the road to the cemetery and walked up the stone steps to the top of the hill where the sanatorium was located. They always met outside, accompanied by a nurse. The last time he was brought out in a wheelchair to avoid overtaxing him. Doris felt increasing alarm as Philip's condition seemed to worsen, although she never said anything.

William Braun continued to come by to help, but not as often. He was busy at the firehouse, and he was also seeing a new lady friend.

Will said one day, "Her name is Mary, and she lives on the North side, not far from me. Her mother and mine know each other, and we met at a church supper. We've been seeing each other on my days off."

Doris was somewhat taken aback but quickly realized she shouldn't have been surprised. After all, Will was close to thirty, and she knew he had hoped to meet someone.

She said, "I'm glad you've met someone nice. I wish you the best, and I know Philip will be pleased, too."

"Yes," he said, "I've already written to him about Mary."

Doris kept in close touch with Helen Shore, often visiting in the evening. They sometimes went to the movies and, on Helen's day off, would spend the afternoon downtown shopping. They didn't buy much, but they liked looking in the stores and admiring the pretty clothes on display in the windows. Doris liked to imagine herself wearing them. They always ended the day at the Japanese Tea Room at Schrafft's. They loved the elegance of the cafe with its white tablecloths and china cups. They would enjoy a cup of tea and a piece of cake or pie or sometimes treat themselves to a hot fudge sundae. Doris always stopped at the candy shop to take home a small bag of chocolates for Arnette.

One day, Helen said, "A few of us are going to a speakeasy this week."

Doris said, "Oh, I've heard about the speakeasies! What are they like?"

"Well," Helen said, "Do you remember Tom Hollingsworth from school?"

Doris nodded in anticipation.

Then Helen said, "Well, he works with me at the bank, and we're friends. He's been there and told me a lot about them. You have to knock on the door and say something like *Hello, Nelly* to be let in. Then, there are drinks and music where you can dance."

Doris said, "Oh, that sounds like fun. Do you think I could go?"

Helen said, "Sure, a group of us are going. I think you probably know some of them; they're from around Elmwood."

Doris left the house that evening, dressed up in one of her favorite dresses and wearing her pretty black dancing shoes. Louise had agreed to mind the girls, but Doris only told her that she and Helen were going to a party with some friends from school. Helen picked Doris up in her father's car, and the two set off for a night of adventure and fun. Doris was unfamiliar with where they were going, but Helen seemed to know the way. They drove down a dark street and drove up to a curb, where they saw a group of people standing under a street light near a building. Doris saw Tom Hollingsworth and also recognized a few others she had known from school.

The group entered the building and walked up a few flights of stairs. They knocked on a door and, after giving a password, found themselves in a brightly lit room crowded with people. Music was playing, and everyone looked like they were having fun. Doris smiled as she took in the view. Their friend, Tom, told Doris and Helen that he would get them a drink from the bar. He soon returned with a gin fizz for each of them. Doris sat at a small table, sipping it. She rarely drank alcoholic beverages and could feel the effect immediately going to her head. Doris smiled and tapped her toes to the music. One of the young men at the table asked her to dance, and after only a brief hesitation, she stood up and extended her hand. Soon, she was swaying and twirling around the dance floor.

Doris had always loved to dance, but it had been a long time since she had done so. In no time, she was dancing around the floor, remembering the way she had danced at her school dances and the steps she had learned from Helen as they danced to the ragtime music on the phonograph.

The song had no sooner ended when another young man asked her to dance. This continued all evening and before she knew it, Helen was telling her it was time to leave. Doris couldn't remember having so much fun.

Louise was still awake and remarked on the late hour. Doris told her only that she had seen some people at the party that she hadn't seen in a long time and enjoyed catching up with them. Of course, she mentioned nothing about the speakeasy or her consumption of alcohol, both of which Louise would have greatly disapproved.

She also decided not to say anything about it to Philip in her next letter. Doris faithfully wrote to Philip telling him of all the events happening in their lives, but there were times when it was better to omit some things.

Doris always gave an accounting of all news of the girls, and Philip looked forward to those letters. Not only did he enjoy hearing all the news, but time often passed very slowly in the sanatorium, and he was grateful for the brief reprieve the letters provided. He also was glad to hear from Will Braun and an occasional letter from Louise Bowman. He hadn't heard from his mother in a while and was impatient to hear news of the farm.

Finally, Charlie wrote on August 1, 1922.

Dear Phil,
I'm sorry I haven't written in so long, but everything has been kind of up in the air. I finally have some news to tell you. I think I told you that things hadn't been going well on the farm. Well, everything

continued to go from bad to worse. We didn't think we could make the payment on the mortgage and thought about trying to get it extended, even though it would cost us more interest.

Then two things happened. The first thing was our neighbor, Mr. Van Sickle, told us he had lost his hired man, asking if he knew anyone he could hire. Then, we got an offer to buy our farm. So, that was it!

As you know, the Van Sickles have a large farm with quite a few acres as well as several heads of cows that need to be milked every day. Even with Mr. Van Sickle's son, he still couldn't manage alone. There is a small house on the property, and Mother and Claude said Mr. Van Sickle told them they could live there rent-free along with a small salary. The house is big enough for them, along with Agnes. So, they sold the farm and seem to be happy enough living there.

There wasn't room for me, and I was glad enough to leave. I've had enough of the farm. I now live in town with Grandmother and Grandpa. I think I told you that I've learned to drive a motorcar and have been doing extra work repairing other people's cars. I'm getting pretty good at it. I now have a job at O'Leary's garage. I'm learning even more and hope to become a real mechanic.

I've been saving some money and may get up to Syracuse one of these days. There is an old Oldsmobile made in the factory here in Lansing sitting in the corner of the garage. I've been tinkering with it, trying to get it going again. Mr. O'Leary said he might give me a good price for it. I've thought about it, but will probably use my thumb to hitch a ride. I've talked to some people and have some maps, so I think I can do it. So maybe you will be seeing me one of these days.

Your brother,
Charlie

Philip wrote on August 14, 1922

Dear Charlie,

I was surprised to hear the news about the farm, but it's just as well. They have struggled for a long time trying to save it. After I heard from you, I wrote a letter to Mother. I expect to hear from her before long.

I'm glad you are well out of it. I know you hated the farm as much as I did. I hope you make it up to Syracuse. I've already written to Doris, and she will be happy to see you. She talked to her parents, and they agreed to let you stay with them while you are here. I'll be waiting to hear from you.

Your brother,
Phil

CHAPTER 26

Doris opened the door and saw Charlie standing on the porch. One hand was holding his violin case, and the other was slung over his shoulder, carrying a beat-up canvas bag. Doris stood aside as Charlie stepped over the threshold and relieved of his possessions, they both looked at each other.

"Charlie, I knew you were coming but didn't expect you this soon."

"Yes, I made better time than I thought I would. I hitched rides with motorcars, wagons, and even a couple of trucks. Before I knew it, I was in Syracuse and found my way to your house."

"Well, come in. You must be ready to sit for a while and have a cool drink."

Charlie sat at the kitchen table as Doris went to the faucet and drew a glass of cold water. They sat together, and Doris smiled as she listened to the adventures Charlie had experienced on the road. *He looks so much like Philip.* She had greatly anticipated his visit. Although she didn't know him well, she liked him very much. His easy going manner and good humor would make for a pleasant change. She also felt that seeing Charlie would pick up Philip's spirits, as he seemed especially downhearted of late.

Doris said, "I'm so glad you're here, and I know Philip will be happy to see you. He talked of nothing else in his last letter."

"Yes," he said, "I can't wait to see him. It's been almost three years. When do you think we can go?"

"We can try to go tomorrow. No visitors are allowed in the sanatorium, but if the weather is good, a nurse can bring Philip outside, and we can talk to him there. It's a bit of a walk to the sanatorium. I imagine you're tired, so tomorrow will be better. I'll call my mother and tell her you're here. They're expecting you. You can stay in my old room."

They heard sounds from one of the bedrooms, and they heard "Mama" called out. Arnette then entered the kitchen and looked around, her eyes landing on Charlie.

Doris said, "She just woke up from her nap." Then to Arnette, "This is your Uncle Charlie, he's your daddy's brother."

Charlie said, "Hello, Arnette. I've been waiting to meet you." To Doris, he said, "She's so pretty. She looks just like Phil."

Doris smiled, "Yes, she does."

The next morning, the two headed to the Sanatorium, crossing the road and walking through the cemetery and up the stone steps in order to reach the sanatorium. The weather was pleasantly warm, and they walked as they talked. Doris said, "Did you find your room comfortable?"

"Yes," he said. "I went out like a light and never heard a thing until it was morning. I had a good supper, too. Your mother sure is a good cook."

Doris smiled, "Yes, she's much better than I am, although she has tried to teach me."

When they reached the building, they entered the administration office and spoke to a clerk.

Doris said, "We would like to see my husband. Would it be possible to bring him out?"

"Have you made an appointment?"

"Well, no. Mr. Boughton's brother has just come to town, and he hasn't seen him in a long time."

The clerk frowned, "Well, I'll call and see if it can be arranged.

Please sit down." She pointed to a small row of chairs along the wall.

The two sat and watched as the clerk used the telephone and went to speak to someone in another office. After a time, she said that arrangements would be made, but "It will be a while for someone to bring him down."

They both nodded.

"In the future, it would be better if you did call to make an appointment. The nurses are very busy, and you were lucky that we could accommodate you. We may not be able to do that next time."

Both nodded with ample gratitude. After waiting almost two hours, they were told by the clerk to wait outside and Philip would be brought out. They waited outside and watched as a nurse pushed Philip in a wheelchair.

"He can't walk?" Charlie said.

"I think they're trying to save his energy, but I'm not sure."

Philip smiled when he saw Charlie. "So, you made it! I'm glad to see you."

Charlie smiled, "How are you feeling?"

"Not too bad. How was your road trip?"

"It was good. I'll tell you all about it sometime."

"I'll bet you'll have a lot to tell me. Say, have you met my two girls?"

"Yes, I couldn't wait to meet them – poor Arnette, she looks just like you." Then laughed, "Just kidding, she's very pretty. So is Beverly. You lucky dog!"

Philip wanted to know how the Osborns were doing.

"They seem to be settling in. I saw them not long before I left, and everything seemed to be OK. Our half-sister Agnes is almost one now. They sure seem to love her."

They talked for a while until the nurse told them it was time to end the visit. "We don't want to tire him."

After saying their goodbyes, they walked home, both lost in their thoughts and not saying much about the visit.

A few days later, they sat on the porch, enjoying the late September weather. Charlie offered Doris a cigarette, and she accepted it. Doris had begun smoking after Philip came home from the war, at first taking an occasional cigarette from his package. After Philip entered the sanatorium, she began purchasing her own. Philip hadn't minded that she smoked, but her mother greatly disapproved. She thought it was a dirty habit and "unladylike." Doris didn't pay much attention to that. Many women were now smoking, and she felt it relaxed her.

As they sat smoking, not much was said until Charlie said, "Do you think Phil is getting better?"

Doris paused, "I don't know."

Charlie said, "I can remember how strong he was. Now, he looks so weak and thin. He's been in that place for over a year. How long will it take for him to get better."

Doris said, "I've spoken to his doctor, but he never seems to say much."

Of course, Doris had watched Philip's decline throughout his illness, but it must have been quite a shock for Charlie, not having seen him in a long time.

Doris only said, "We can only hope that one day he will improve."

They made another visit later in the fall with the same disappointing outcome.

As winter began to close in, they had to discontinue the visits.

Charlie looked for employment and began working at a garage on South Avenue. The Bowmans were happy to have him stay on with them, and they agreed on a small weekly fee for room and board. Charlie worked most days, either walking to and from work or taking the streetcar. He usually ate supper with Louise and Horace, but then later would often drift over to spend the evening with Doris and the girls. The two adults would often play checkers or backgammon, and Charlie sometimes told Arnette stories about growing up on the farm. He often brought along his violin, filling the room with sweet-sounding music, delighting the girls. Arnette loved dancing around the room as Beverly smiled from her mother's lap.

He came over one evening a few days before Christmas. Doris was busy cleaning up after supper. Arnette sat at the table drawing a picture to send to her father, and Beverly sat on a small rug playing with some toys.

Charlie said to Arnette, "Would you like to go and see Santa Claus?"

Arnette's eyes widened, "Santa Claus?"

Doris walked over to the table with a questioning look.

Charlie then pulled a newspaper clipping from his pocket.

Doris looked at it and read, "Santa Claus will be at Edwards Department Store this Saturday. Come and meet Santa and receive a toy from him!!"

Arnette said, "Oh, can we go?"

Doris said, "I think Uncle Charlie has already decided we will go."

The following Saturday, the three boarded a streetcar and headed to E.W. Edwards Department Store. When they entered the toy department, they found a long line of children waiting to see Santa Claus. They waited for what seemed like hours, and Arnette became restless at times, "When will I see Santa Claus?" she said several times.

At last, she climbed up on Santa's lap, and with a merry ho-ho-ho, he asked if she had been a good girl. Arnette nodded, and Santa reached into his bag and gave her a small cloth doll and a peppermint stick.

They then joined the throng of shoppers on the sidewalk. Garlands and lights were strung along the streets, and the store windows were decorated for Christmas. They walked to St. Mary's Circle and saw the fifty-foot evergreen tree that had, just a few days ago, been transported to the circle in readiness for the Christmas Eve tree lighting celebration. They ended the afternoon with a trip to Schrafft's for ice cream.

A few days later, Horace and Charlie appeared with a Christmas tree purchased on the sidewalk outside a shop on South Avenue. Doris hadn't put up a tree for the last two years. The months and years as she watched Philip suffer through his long illness and then enter the sanatorium had been difficult and lonely. The loneliness wore her down, and she found she had no desire or will for these festivities. Last year, Doris and the girls had celebrated with the Bowmans. Now, as the air filled the room with the fragrance of the scented conifer, she began to feel like the spirit of Christmas. On Christmas Eve, Charlie helped Doris and Arnette decorate the tree.

The winter was cold and snowy. A big storm in February brought even the streetcars to a halt as citizens were needed to clear the tracks. Doris was snowed in more than once, but Charlie and the neighborhood men helped to clear the snow. Winter nights were spent playing games, singing, and telling stories. Sometimes, they made popcorn on the stove. Philip was often in their thoughts, imagining him lying in a cold bed next to the open window as the wind blew over him. They felt helpless to do anything apart from their frequent letters.

At last, Spring arrived, and on one of the first warm days, they walked up the hill to visit Philip. Doris had made an appointment, and the nurse was ready as he was wheeled out again in a wheelchair.

After they greeted him, Philip immediately said, "I want to go home. Please take me home. I'm not getting any better here. I want to go home."

Doris hesitated, then said, "I'll make an appointment and see what the doctor says." Doris had spoken to Philip's doctor, Dr. Taylor, a few times and she had usually found him to be reasonable and willing to listen to her. When the visit with Philip ended, Doris made an appointment with Dr. Taylor for the following week.

Later, Doris found the telephone number for Dr. Benjamin Green and placed a call to him. Dr. Green later returned her call, and he remembered Philip.

"How is he doing in the Sanatorium"?

Doris spoke of Philip's present condition, "Philip wants to come home. He doesn't feel he's getting any better in the Sanatorium. I'm sure that the doctors won't want him to come home. I want to do what's best, but I don't know what to do."

Dr. Green said, "I don't believe he should leave the sanatorium. For one thing, he's contagious, and you will place yourself and anyone else in the home at risk. It often takes a long time to cure tuberculosis, sometimes years."

"For years?" she said.

"Yes, I'm sorry to say that it is, and the sanatorium is the best place for him to be, but he may do better in another hospital."

Doris listened. "Another hospital? But where?"

I'm thinking of the Oswego County Sanatorium in Orwell. It's about fifty miles from here, and it's located in a rural area where the air is fresh and clean. I've recently visited the place and was given a tour. I was impressed with the cleanliness and cheerful atmosphere. The food is also very good. I was told they have recently added several more beds in order to allow for those who live outside Oswego County. I'm going to see if it can be arranged."

When Doris kept the appointment with Dr. Taylor, she was informed that he had already spoken to Dr. Green.

Although he wasn't happy, he would be agreeable, "If that's

what you want." He said, "We believe our care is very good, but if that's what you want and if your husband agrees, it can be done. You will be notified when a bed is available."

It took some convincing for Philip to agree to yet another sanatorium. He wanted badly to go home, but in the end, he was convinced it was for the best. In late August, Doris received a letter from the Onondaga County Health Department informing her that a bed had become available and Philip would be admitted to the Oswego County Sanatorium. On September 1, 1923, he left the Onondaga County Sanatorium and was transported to Orwell.

In September, Charlie received a letter from his mother.

September 10, 1923

Dear Charlie.

I'm afraid that Claude has met with an accident. While climbing up the ladder on a silo, he missed his footing and fell to the ground. He had a hard fall and broke one of his arms. He isn't able to work, and we are living with your grandparents. Mr. Van Sickle is now looking for a hired man. I told him that you might be able to come back and work the farm until Claude gets better. We don't want to lose our place there. Please let me know as soon as possible because Mr. Van Sickle is waiting for an answer.

With love,
Mother

Charlie hated the thought of returning to the farm, but he felt he had no choice. There was no one else, so he wrote to his mother, telling her that he would return as soon as he could.

When he told Doris, she was somewhat surprised but probably

shouldn't have been. She always knew Charlie would leave some-day but had somehow hoped he never would. Doris had never known life as anything other than that of an only child, but for a short time, she had felt she'd had a brother, and now it seemed that would come to an end.

Now she said, "I'll be sorry to see you leave, but I understand. You've been here a long time. You must be missing your family and friends."

"Yes, I'm missing people there, and I miss my home. I like it here, but I guess I'll always be a Michigan boy." He then said with a smile, " I may get back here one of these days."

"I hope so," she said.

Charlie gave his notice at the garage, and a few days later, he gathered up his belongings and said goodbye to the Bowmans. When he was ready to leave, Doris and the girls were already wait-ing in the yard for him. He kissed both the girls, and then he and Doris wrapped their arms around each other. He picked up his violin case and carryall bag and, with a wave, turned and walked down the road. Doris watched until he was out of sight.

Arnette said, "I'll miss Uncle Charlie."

"Yes," she said, I'll miss him too."

Then they slowly turned and walked into the house.

CHAPTER 27

October 30, 1923

Dear Doris,

I've been given permission to raise the head of my bed more than usual in order to write this letter. As I've told you, my earlier letters were written by a nurse. Except for a short time when I'm eating, I'm required to spend the rest of the time flat on my back. I am even fed by the nurses, as they don't want me to use any needed exertion.

My bed is on the porch, and for the first time, I'm able to raise my head enough to see the hills in the distance. Today is a sunny day, and I can see the beautiful colors of the autumn trees. They won't last long. They are falling quickly, and soon, the trees will be bare.

There is already a chill in the air, and I've heard the winters are very cold and snowy here, even more so than at home. I do see a couple of patients out walking around on the grounds. I'm not allowed to get out of bed and move around.

There really is nothing to occupy my mind, and the time passes very slowly. The nurses are nice, and when they have extra time, they sometimes sit for a few minutes and talk to me. Sometimes, I talk to a man in the next bed, but conversation isn't encouraged. We're told not to use up any extra energy. Most of the time, I'm forced to spend my time looking up at the ceiling, finally drifting off to sleep. I can only hope that this is all for a good cause.

I miss you and the girls very much. I wish I could see you but, at present, that isn't possible. I received your letters and also heard from my mother. I finally got a letter from Charlie. He's back on the farm, though not happy about it. I'm sorry he had to do that. He enjoyed his time with you and the girls and hopes to get back there one of these days.

The nurse has told me to end this letter and return to lying flat on my back.

Love,
Philip

Doris read Philip's letter and could only imagine what life must be like in the sanatorium. Would she be able to lie flat on her back, day in and day out, not even being able to talk? What was it like to have someone provide all one's needed care, even having one's food spooned into one's mouth?

Doris wondered if Philip had nightmares like he had at home when he would sometimes dream he was back at the front. Philip never talked much about the war, at least not to her. He thought he may have talked about it with Will Braun, who had also seen action in the war.

Doris hadn't seen Will in a long time. She supposed he was busy with his lady friend and his job at the fire department. Philip once mentioned getting a short note from him.

It had been almost two months since Charlie had been gone, and his absence had left a great void in her life. She thought wistfully of the many evenings they had spent playing board games or just talking. There were times when, without thinking, she would hear a sound and was sure she heard his quick rap on the door and waited for him to call out but, immediately realized it was only the wind.

Doris filled her time as best she could. She had never been someone who enjoyed needlework or other hobbies. She did like to read and frequently visited the library. She spent time with her girls and made daily visits to her mother. Of course, she saw Helen Shore often and kept in touch with her other friends. Many of them were now married and were busy with children.

Doris looked at the calendar on the wall and realized that Thanksgiving would soon be here, and then Christmas would be upon them. She thought about the holidays, once again without Philip here. As she added on her fingers, she realized that of the six years they had known each other, they had only spent two Christmases together. Charlie had been here last year, and he made the holidays fun. This year will be different.

She got out her pen and writing paper, intending to write a letter to Philip, but found she had nothing to say. She had written so many letters, and it seemed she had run out of words. She got up and walked over to the window. She smiled as she looked at the white lace curtains. She had gradually replaced some of the furnishings that had been in the house when they moved in. Doris had an eye for style and beauty and added touches to make the house more pleasant. In the spring and summer, she often picked flowers from the garden and filled them with vases, placing them around the house. Although there was no one else to see them – other than her parents or Helen, she rarely had company these days – looking at them made her feel better.

Now she looked out the window and saw that it had started to rain. *That will undoubtedly bring down the rest of the leaves. It won't be long before it will be winter.* She heard sounds from the bedroom. Arnette was waking from her afternoon nap. As Doris looked at the clock, she saw that it was still early. Arnette was out growing her nap and would be starting school next year.

Doris saw a few photographs on the table near the window,

her father having brought them over this morning. They had been taken with Horace's Brownie camera, and he recently had the roll of film developed. The photographs were of Doris and the two girls outside their house. Doris smiled as she saw the pictures and thought about how happy Philip would be to get them. She would be sure to send them off in her next letter.

⚔

"I have some mail for you, Mr. Boughton; I think one is from your wife."

Philip looked up as the maid, Miss Clarke, handed him the letter. He then said, "I haven't seen you for a while. I wondered where you'd been."

She said, "I had some time off over the Christmas holidays, and I went home to visit my family."

He said, "That must have been nice, but I'm glad to see you back."

Miss Clarke was the regular maid on his ward and she delivered mail and meal trays as well as keeping the rooms clean. She also assisted the nurse with tasks such as bed making and bathing as well as any errands that were needed.

Miss Clarke started working on the ward soon after Philip's arrival and the two had immediately taken a liking to each other. Philip found her to be well-spoken and intelligent. She reminded him a lot of Doris, being small with dark hair that she wore in a short bob. Unlike Doris, Miss Clarke's eyes were hazel, and she had a sprinkling of freckles across her nose.

Over time, they learned the details of their lives. Miss Clarke was from Oswego and had attended the Normal School there but had to leave to take a job. Her father had suddenly died, leaving his widow and several children. A family friend had encouraged her to apply for employment at the sanatorium. With that reference, she was able to obtain employment and not only received her room and board but was able to send money home to her family. She very much hoped to return to school, as her wish was to become a school teacher.

Philip told her about attending the Normal School in Michigan after leaving one year to join the army. He told her about his job at the typewriter company and about his wife and daughters. Miss Clarke had admired the recent photographs of Doris and the girls that he had recently received.

One day, Philip asked what her first name was, and she told him, "It's Eleanor, after my grandmother."

As Philip repeated it to himself, he thought it had a sweet, gentle sound, much like her. "It suits you," he said, "May I call you that?"

She hesitated momentarily but then said, "Yes, if you like."

Thereafter, he began calling her Eleanor, although she continued to call him by his surname, Mr. Boughton.

The two found they had much in common. Both enjoyed reading, and Eleanor always inquired about which book he was reading at the time. When Philip spoke of the effort it was to hold up a book while lying flat on his back, she sympathized, "Maybe I could read to you sometimes,"

"Yes, that would be nice, I'd like that."

Eleanor asked her supervisor if that would be allowed, and she was told that as long as she finished her other tasks, it would be fine. She began finding time each day to read, usually in the later afternoon when most of the other work had been done.

When she asked what he would like to read, he showed her some books that Doris had sent him. "Oh, these are all good. I see one is an Agatha Christie mystery. That would be a good one to start with."

After they had finished that, she visited the hospital library, seeking out any books that Philip might enjoy. They read *Main Street*, and Eleanor found a copy of *Moby Dick* on the shelf. Eleanor was a good reader, and she had a pleasant voice. As Philip listened, he was able to lose himself in the story and, for a short time, forget about the sanatorium.

It was a long winter. As the weather grew colder, his bed was moved back off the porch during the night, but he was still required to spend several hours during the daylight hours on the porch. He was given thick flannel pajamas and his bed layered with warm blankets. He was still confined to his bed, and a physical therapist visited him often to exercise his limbs. Philip had no appetite for food and had to be coaxed to eat.

Philip greatly anticipated the daily reading sessions and began looking around the ward for Eleanor to appear. If she was busy with other tasks and unable to read, he felt great disappointment. He liked looking at her, and although he never touched her, he wished he could. He imagined her lying beside him in bed with their arms around each other. The thought of that could bring tears to his eyes. It had been so long since he had felt the closeness of a woman. He dearly loved Doris, but it had been so long since he had seen her that there were times when he could barely remember what she looked like.

On a day late in April, Eleanor closed the book they were reading. She then said, "Next week will be my last day on this ward."

Philip looked up, surprised by this news, "What do you mean?"

"I've been transferred to the children's building," she said. "I'm told I'll be able to assist the teacher at the school. It's what I've been hoping to do."

Philip didn't know what to say. He wanted to tell her that he didn't want her to leave, but of course, that wouldn't do at all. He could see how happy she was. He only said, "I'll miss you, but I'm glad for you. I know you really want to become a teacher." Then he said, "I hope you'll visit me sometimes."

"Yes, of course," she said, "I'll try to do that."

They said their goodbyes, and that was the last time they spoke.

Philip now spent all his time on the porch. On one of the days that his head was raised, he caught sight of Eleanor in the yard supervising a game with a group of children. He watched her for a time, and he tried to catch her eye, but she took no notice of him.

They found themselves in an area of rolling hills and farm country and finally saw a sign announcing the Oswego County Sanatorium. They turned down the road and were confronted with two large white buildings and a scattering of smaller ones. As they sat in front of the buildings, they saw that the two larger ones were lined with screened porches.

Doris said, "That must be where Philip sleeps."

Doris had written to the sanatorium asking for permission to visit Philip and, at the same time, request an appointment with his doctor. She received a reply, scheduling an appointment with Dr. Hughes, his present physician. She was also told that arrangements would be made to visit Philip.

After consulting a map and determining the route and mileage to Orwell, Doris and her father, Horace Bowman, set out early that morning. The trip was long, consisting of many country roads. They lost their way a couple of times, needing to ask directions, but finally arrived at the sanatorium.

As they found their way into the parking area, Doris said, "It's almost time for our appointment."

They were directed to the administration building and soon found themselves in a small room, awaiting the doctor. Doris felt somewhat anxious, not quite knowing what to expect. She fidgeted in her chair, and her mouth felt dry. Although it was a mild spring day, she felt beads of perspiration on her forehead and neck. The letters she had received from Philip didn't sound hopeful that his condition was improving, and she was apprehensive about what the doctor would say.

Finally, they were called into the doctor's office. They sat at a desk as Dr. Hughes reviewed Philip's records and X-rays. Doris listened to all this without completely understanding all she heard, but she was aware that things were not good with Philip. It appeared his condition had worsened, and they were told by Dr. Hughes that the tuberculosis had now spread to his other lung.

Doris sat staring at the doctor, finally saying, "Is there nothing that can be done?"

Dr. Hughes sadly nodded his head, "We're doing everything we can."

Doris thought about the long years Philip had already spent in the sanatorium, to no avail, and now it seemed things would go on as they were. Doris stumbled out of the office, hardly aware of where she was going. She and Horace were directed to the main building and waited on the screened porch for Philip to be wheeled out.

When Doris saw him, she was shocked at how much thinner and paler he was than she had last seen him, but Philip smiled when he saw them.

"I miss you so much," he said, stopping to catch his breath, then said, "You look so pretty." "Hello, Dad," he said to Horace, "I like the pictures you sent. You're becoming a good photographer."

The effort of talking brought on an episode of coughing. After it had subsided, he said to Doris, "I like seeing the photos of the girls. They're getting so big."

"Yes," she said, "Arnette will start school in the fall."

They spent a short time visiting until the nurse told them it was time to leave. As they prepared to leave, Philip's expression wore a desperate look and he appeared ready to cry. As he left, Doris could see that the back of his head was nearly bald, probably due to constant lying on his back.

After they left the building, they found a bench and sat for a time. Doris had controlled her tears during the visit but was now unable to hold them back, and she cried quietly for several minutes.

Horace watched her helplessly and finally reached over to

lightly pat her knee. "It'll be OK," he said, "What will be, will be." Horace was a rather stoic man and not given to demonstrative emotions.

Doris only nodded. They sat for a while, Doris staring at the white buildings with their screened porches. In one of them, she knew that Philip was confined to his bed, and she was hesitant to leave. She knew it would be a long time before she saw him again, if ever. Finally, they made their way to their car. Doris had brought some sandwiches and they stopped near the Salmon River to have their lunch, but Doris ate only a few bites, having no appetite for food. The trip back to Syracuse was long and mostly devoid of conversation.

CHAPTER 28

September had been unseasonably cold with frequent heavy rain, and a few times, Doris noticed frost on the ground outside her window. Arnette now walked to and from school, bundled up in a warm sweater, raincoat, and boots.

With the turn of a calendar page, October unfolded into a warm Indian summer that lasted for several days. Doris and Helen sat on the porch, savoring the sunshine as they enjoyed lemonade and cookies. Doris hadn't seen Helen in a while. She was working more hours at the bank, having been given more responsibility that came along with a new promotion. Today, however, she had a day off, and the two women were catching up on what was happening in their lives.

Helen wanted to know how Philip was doing. "I wrote a letter to him a couple of weeks ago but haven't heard from him in a while."

Doris explained that "it's hard for him to write letters because he has to lie flat most of the time, and the short time he's allowed to sit, I guess he saves those times for writing to me and to his mother."

"Have you been able to visit him?"

"Not since Spring," Doris said. "I've called the sanatorium but I am told he isn't allowed to have visitors at this time. We aren't allowed in the hospital, and Philip isn't able to get out of bed."

"Do they give you reports?" Helen said. "About his condition, I mean."

"Yes," Doris said. "Sometimes, I'm able to talk to a doctor. I do know he isn't doing well. I worry about him all the time. All I can do is write letters to him. He's always happy to get them and the photographs I send of the girls. He misses them terribly."

Helen said, "How does Arnette like school?"

"Oh, she loves going to school. She walks there with a group of neighborhood children and can't wait to go each day. She's learning all her letters and wants very badly to learn to read."

They talked about people they knew, and then Helen asked about Will Braun. "You haven't mentioned him in a while.."

"No," she said. "I guess he's busy working at the fire department – that and he has a lady friend. I haven't heard from him in a while. I think Philip does hear from him now and then."

Doris wrote:
October 15, 1924

Dear Philip,
After a cold, rainy September, we are continuing to have warm, sunny weather. Helen came over today, and we were able to sit out on the Porch. Helen really likes her job, and the bank seems to like her as well. She was recently given a promotion. She's a real career girl.

Arnette loves school. They had a Meet the Teachers Day, and I was able to meet Arnette's teacher, Miss Crandall. She told me that Arnette is very smart and well-behaved in school. Arnette likes her school, Elmwood Elementary, and she has made a lot of new friends. I think I told you that I went to that same school as a young girl, and it seemed strange imagining our daughter may be sitting in the same classroom. Arnette told me a photographer took a picture of the class, but she didn't know if we would be given one of the pictures.

I have called the sanatorium but am still told that I'm not permitted to visit. I miss you very much. My parents send their regards to you as well.

Love,
Doris

⚯

Doris sniffed the air as she became gradually aware of the odor of smoke. Looking around, she thought, *Did I leave a cigarette burning?*

She suddenly heard loud voices, followed by a sharp knock on the door. As Doris ran to the door, she saw her neighbor, Mr. Schaefer, looking very excited.

"There's a fire! Get your girls and get outside."

The girls had been playing in their room, and both adults ran, picking up Beverly and Doris taking Arnette by the hand, as they quickly exited the front door. The air was filled with smoke, and as Doris looked up, she gasped and saw flames coming from the roof.

Mr. Schaefer said, "I think someone behind you was burning leaves, and some of the cinders caught the wind and landed on your roof.

Doris and the girls huddled on the lawn, joined by other neighbors watching the spectacle. Doris heard sirens and then saw a fire engine drive up. The men pulled the hose out, and before long, the fire was out. Doris heard a familiar voice, and as he removed his helmet, she recognized Will Braun.

"Why Will, I haven't seen you in so long."

He said, "I heard the alarm come in, and I thought it might be your house. I'm glad you and the girls are alright."

They stood talking, and another man joined them. "I'm John Hogan. I work with Will at the station. It looks like your house is okay; just some burned shingles, but everything is out now. Still, it would be a good idea not to sleep here tonight, just to make sure. Do you have someplace else where you can sleep?

"Yes," she said. "I can stay with my parents."

"Good," he said. "I'll have an inspector come by and check the house. If everything passes the inspection, you can move back in."

The firemen took their leave, and Doris was soon joined by the Bowmans. They helped her gather up the things they would need for the night.

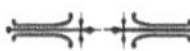

A few days later, when Doris and the girls were back in their house, she heard a knock on the door. As she opened it, she was surprised to find Will Braun standing there.

"Hello," she said with a smile, "Please come in."

"I wanted to see how you are doing?" He said. "It seems you didn't experience much damage to your house."

"No," she said. "We were lucky. A few shingles were burned, but my father knows someone who can repair them. Please sit down, Will; I haven't seen you in so long."

"Yes, it's good to see you. How is Phil doing?"

"Not well, I'm afraid. I haven't been able to visit him for a while. I get reports from the doctor. He has some good days, but mostly, he seems to be doing poorly. I don't know what will happen."

"That's terrible! I hate to hear that."

They heard the door close. Doris said, "Arnette is home from school."

Arnette looked at Will, and Doris said, "Do you remember Mr. Braun, Daddy's friend?"

Arnette nodded and smiled.

"Hello, Arnette," he said. "I can't believe you are in school already."

"Yes," she said. "I'm learning to read now."

Will said, "What about the baby, Beverly? She must be getting big."

Doris said, "She's taking her nap now. She's three."

"I can hardly believe it. I remember when she was first born."

Doris said, "Would you like to come over and have supper with us sometime? The girls would love to have company. My cooking still isn't the best, but I can manage to prepare an acceptable meal."

"Oh, I seem to remember you made some pretty good meals," he said. "Yes, I'd like to come. I'll check with the firehouse to see what my schedule looks like, and then I'll call you."

Later, she sat down and wrote a letter to Philip. She wrote about the weather they were having and what Arnette was doing in school. She talked about going to the park with the girls and other news of the day. She decided not to tell him about the fire as he would only worry about it. After all, no one was injured, and it appeared there was no damage to the house.

She also decided she wouldn't mention Will's visit and her invitation to supper.

Doris roasted a chicken and prepared some potatoes and vegetables.

Will said, "This is very good – much better than I'm used to at the firehouse."

As they ate, Doris asked about Will's lady friend, Mary. "You haven't mentioned her. How are things going with her?"

He said, "I'm no longer seeing her. I guess we weren't right for each other. It was mostly our mothers who wanted us to get together, and you know how that is."

Nothing more was said about it, and after supper, Doris suggested that Will read the girls a story while she cleaned up the kitchen. Later, they sat and talked for a time as the girls played together on the floor.

Finally, Doris told the girls to go and brush their teeth and get ready for bed. "I'll be in to tuck you in and say good night."

Will said, "I have to be going; I'm on duty later tonight."

Arnette said, "Can you come back again?"

Doris turned to Will and said, "We'll have you over again. It's been too long since we saw you."

The girls went to get ready for bed, and as Will left, he said, "Arnette asked me if she could call me Uncle Will. I said it was Okay. I hope you don't mind."

"No," she said. "She still misses her Uncle Charlie terribly, and of course, she misses her father."

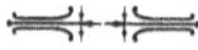

January 1, 1925

Dear Philip,

Here it is, the start of a new year. It's hard to realize another year has again gone by. We had a quiet Christmas but we managed to celebrate what we could. The girls wanted a Christmas tree and my father brought one over and set it up in the living room. The girls helped me decorate it.

We already had a big snowstorm, and we now have a lot of snow in our yard. The girls, along with the neighborhood children, have been having fun making snowballs and snowmen. My father bought the girls a sled for Christmas and the older children like to pull the younger ones around through the snow.

I hope you liked the books I sent you. One is an Agatha Christie mystery; I remembered you enjoyed the other one I sent you. My father took some new photographs of the girls outside playing in the snow, and I'll send them to you when he has them developed. I'll also send some to your mother.

I called the sanatorium and spoke to a nurse (I think it was a nurse, but it may have been someone like a secretary). She did say that there hasn't been much change.

> *I miss you and always, your loving wife,*
> *Doris*

Philip read Doris's letter. He had difficulty writing letters now but the nurses are usually agreeable to writing a short letter for him. If they had time, they sometimes read to him. He missed the daily reading sessions with Eleanor. He wondered how she was. He had asked some of the other maids and nurses but they always said they didn't know.

Winter had set in with a vengeance. He heard the wind blowing fiercely and saw the drifting snow as it whipped up in the air. He now slept inside at night, but he was required to spend at least some time on the porch. He stood it as long as he could endure and then rang for the nurse to take him back inside. The days were long and monotonous. He missed Doris so much and longed for his girls. He wondered if they even remembered him.

Doris read Philip's latest letter. She knew it had been written by a nurse. Reading the unfamiliar handwriting made him feel even more distant from her.

Will had become a regular visitor to the house. Doris would prepare supper, and then they would spend time with the girls. After they had gone to bed, Will would remain, and on one of the evenings, he confessed his love for Doris.

"I always loved you from the first day we met," he said. "I know how much you love Philip, and he's my good friend as well, but I can't help feeling the way I do."

Doris had always known that Will had those feelings for her. Now, as he moved closer and put his arms around her, she felt a warm glow. It had been so long since anyone had touched or held her close.

He kissed her and said, "I've wanted to do that for such a long time."

That night, they found their way to Doris's bed, one of many nights they would spend there. Will always left early in the morning, before Arnette got up for school. Doris sometimes wondered if a neighbor had seen him leave. Some of the neighbors were friendly with her mother, and it was possible that one of them would tell Louise, but Doris put it out of her mind. She only knew the pleasure and contentment she felt when Will was holding her closely. She loved Philip and wanted him to get better and come home, but she also realized every day that that probably wouldn't happen.

Philip wrote:
March 30, 1925

Dear Doris,
I seem to have more energy than I have felt in a long time and am sitting with my head raised writing this letter. Last night was a clear night, and as I looked out the window, I could see the sky was filled with stars. Even though it was a very cold night, I asked the nurse if she could wheel my bed out on the porch so I could see the stars. She bundled me up and wheeled me out, and as I looked out, I wondered if you might be looking up, seeing the same stars.

Do you remember the first time we went downtown to see a film together — I don't remember the name of the film, but Mary Pickford was the star. Anyway, we got off the trolley, and as we walked up the hill, we looked up to see the sky was filled with stars, much like it was last night. I still remember the way you looked and the way

*you looked at me. That was our first kiss and the night we fell in
love. So much has happened since then. I love you so much and all
I want is to get back to you and to our girls.*

I'm tired, so I will finish this letter tomorrow.

Philip never finished the letter. He drifted off to sleep, and the letter sat on his bedside table, seeming to have forgotten it was there.
After a few days, a nurse asked if he wanted to mail it.

He seemed somewhat confused but said, "Yes, please do that."

The nurse saw that it was for his wife, and she added a note at
the bottom of the letter and then addressed an envelope and sent
it off to Doris.

That was the last letter Philip ever wrote.

Doris wrote:
April 12, 1925

Dear Philip,
*I got your last letter, and I do remember the night we came home
from the movies and that starry night. I'll never forget it and our
first kiss. That was the first of so many wonderful times we had
together. I'll always remember the Fourth of July picnic at Helen's,
and the day we spent at Long Branch Park – screaming as we clung
to each other, racing down the roller coaster. Most of all, I remember
our wedding and the night we spent at the Cobblestone Inn.*

*It seems that we haven't had times like that for a long time. It
seemed that everything changed after the war. We can only hope
that things will get better and we can have happy times again. I
love you, Philip, and send your love to Arnette and Beverly.*

Love,
Doris

Although Doris kept hoping every day that she would get another letter from Philip, she never received one. She read the letter over and over, unfolding and folding it until it became wrinkled and smudged and then partially illegible, but by that time, Doris had committed the letter to her memory.

Over the next three months, Philip drifted in and out of sleep, sometimes only waking to take in water and nourishment. He was aware of the nurses coming and going, caring for him, but there were other times when he was unaware of his surroundings. He lost sense of time and place. Sometimes, he was back in France or on the farm in Michigan. At other times, he thought of Doris and his daughters, wondering where they were.

Philip was marching toward the train with the rest of his company. The sounds of many heavy feet filled his ears – *stomp, stomp, stomp.* It seemed endless, as if they had been marching forever, marching toward the train that would take him to France and the Western Front.

He was looking for Doris. *She said she would be here,* he thought, but he couldn't see her. "Doris," he called out. "Are you here?"

He lifted his foot to march but had difficulty moving it. He heard a soft voice nearby. "Did you call me, Mr. Boughton? Do you need something?"

Philip opened his eyes and saw a young woman dressed in white looking down at him. It was Miss Ryan, one of the nurses on his ward. He then realized he had been dreaming. He wasn't on his way to the front. The war had been over for several years. He was in the sanatorium where he had been for almost two years. He couldn't remember when he had last been out of bed, much less able to march or even walk.

His body was covered with perspiration as he struggled to breathe. His heart cried out for Doris. It had been so long since he had seen her. Not being allowed visitors, he had been shut away, isolated from everyone he loved. He remembered the last time he saw her. She and her father had made the trip from Syracuse, where they talked through a screen door. She was faithful about writing and giving him the news of their daughters.

Philip wondered how long he would go on as he was – *probably not much longer,* he thought. It had been four years since he learned he had tuberculosis. At first, he'd been hopeful that he would get better, but he eventually came to realize that it was never going to happen. It had been a long struggle, but he realized it was almost over. He now wondered what it was like to die. Like most of the people he knew, church had been a part of his life, but although he had always believed in God, he wasn't especially religious. He had never given a lot of thought to an afterlife. Was it a nice place? Would he and Doris ever meet again at some future time? His thoughts turned to Doris and their two daughters, and he felt his heart break for them. Well, there didn't seem to be anything he could do about it.

The nurse was sponging him and changing his pajamas, then adjusting his pillows. Philip sighed and closed his eyes. He never opened them again. He fell into a deep sleep and died two days later.

"Hello, am I speaking to Mrs. Boughton?" said the voice on the telephone.

"Yes," Doris said, "This is Mrs. Boughton speaking."

"This is Dr. Hollis at the Oswego County Sanatorium."

"Yes, Dr. Hollis, are you calling about my husband?"

"Yes, and I'm afraid I have bad news. Mr. Boughton passed away this morning."

Doris took in the news silently. It was not completely unexpected. She knew that Philip had been failing, but she had continued to cling to a small thread of hope that somehow he would get better.

Dr. Hollis continued to talk. "We have instructions from the Army that his body is to be sent to Marshall, Michigan for burial."

"Yes, that will be fine," Doris said. "Will you notify his mother?"

"Yes, I don't have a telephone number for her."

"No," said Doris. "I'm sorry, I don't know what it is."

"Well, I will notify her by telegram."

Dr. Hollis talked for a few more minutes as Doris listened without really hearing and without saying much until the call ended. She hung up the telephone and stood staring into space before walking over to the window. A tear slid down her cheek as she looked out at her two daughters playing in the yard. She couldn't believe Philip was really gone. She wondered what it was like for him at the end. Was he alone and was he thinking of her?

She thought back to the day she had first met him at the movie house. *What if I hadn't skipped school that day and gone to the movies? We never would have met! What would my life have been like? What will happen to me now?* Her thoughts were in a whirl as she began to cry in earnest.

Her mind went back to the happy times before Philip left for the war. She remembered their wedding supper with Helen and Andy at the Cobblestone Inn, then that same night spent in a room in the same inn. She could still hear the sounds of talk and laughter rising from the first floor and then see the street lamp shining through the window as they lay in each other's arms, making plans for the future when the war was over and Philip was back home.

Most of all, she thought of the way she had felt when they first fell in love, and of course, there were their two beautiful daughters.

They had so many hopes and dreams but it all ended so quickly. Doris stood by the window as she pondered her life and her future.

A few months later, William Braun would ask her to marry him, and she would accept.

Will had a good job and was well able to provide for her and the girls. Being a kind man who truly loved her, he would be a good husband and a father to her children. While Doris would care for Will and try to be a good wife, she would never feel the same passion, that intense joy she had felt with Philip, her first love. Things just hadn't turned out the way she had hoped. She had expected so much more, but what exactly? She didn't know.

Three years later, Doris would also die of tuberculosis, finally bringing their story to a close. As the illness took hold of her mind in those final moments, once again, she returned to that fateful late spring day when she and Helen skipped school, giggling about the handsome soldiers in line at the movie house.

But that future was yet to come, still unknown to Doris on that summer day. She stood looking out the window, her head preoccupied with thoughts of all that could be.

EPILOGUE

Philip died in 1925 at the age of 28 and was buried in the Boughton family plot in Marshall, Michigan. A few months after his death, Doris married William Braun. In less than a year, she became ill with tuberculosis and moved into her mother's home, where Louise became Doris's caregiver. She died in 1928 at the age of 29. William Braun moved on after her death, and the girls never saw or heard from him again. He remarried and died in the VA hospital at the age of 65. After Doris's death, the girls remained in the care of the Bowmans, who doted on them, even purchasing ponies for them. Horace Bowman died of an apparent heart attack in 1930, and Louise died in 1932.

Charlie Boughton remained in Michigan, where he became a mechanic, eventually marrying a woman several years older than him. They never had any children. Charlie died in a Calhoun County sanatorium after a long illness with tuberculosis. He died at age 34. Nothing is known about what became of his widow.

Agnes Osborn died at home at the age of 15 following a Strep infection. Claude and Nellie Osborn lived out their remaining years in Marshall, Michigan, inheriting the home from Nellie's father, Frank Smith. Both lived into their seventies.

Following the death of the Bowmans, the two girls, Arnette and Beverly, became wards of the state, living as foster children with distant relatives. The girls never received the loving care and attention they received from their grandparents, and although they were never mistreated or abused, they often had to work very hard. Both girls graduated from high school, attending North High School in Syracuse and then at Tully High School. Arnette was an especially accomplished student, serving as vice president of her senior class and graduating with honors.

Both girls left home after high school. Beverly married a dairy farmer and eventually had three children. Arnette took a position in Syracuse as a maid in the mansion of the owner of a well-known candle company. She met a young man at a YMCA dance and then married him and had two daughters, one of whom became the author of this book. In her later years, Arnette was employed in the accounting department of a large manufacturing company in Syracuse. She became known as a well-respected, intelligent, hard worker, always willing to learn new tasks and methods. She worked there for several years until her retirement at age 65. Always an avid reader, she joined a book club and was active in many community activities. She was a devoted wife and mother to her husband and daughters. Both Arnette and Beverly had long, happy marriages, living into their senior years while enjoying their children and grandchildren.

AUTHOR'S NOTES AND ACKNOWLEDGEMENTS

When I began writing this book, I had only the bare bones of a story. Both my grandparents, Doris and Philip Boughton, died long before I was born. My mother rarely spoke of them. She was a child when they died, and the details she told me were sparse. When coaxed, she told me stories of Doris's mother being angry after cutting her hair short and raising the hems of her skirts. She also told me that Doris loved to dance, and she referred to her as a flapper. My mother barely remembered her father except for the letters he wrote from the sanatorium.

I will begin by telling you that this book is a work of fiction, and many of the details are themselves fiction. Except for the Boughtons, the Bowmans, and the Osborns, most of the other people in the book are fictional characters (with the exception of a few historical figures like President Wilson and General Pershing). As I constructed my story, I knew that much would need to come from my imagination, but I tried to stay as close as I could to what was true about my grandparents and to the times in which they lived.

I had always known that Philip fought in France during World War I and was gassed. He also spent many years in a sanatorium, and both he and Doris died from tuberculosis. Among the articles I found after my parents died were a photograph of the two of them, Philip's discharge document from the Army, and a few newspaper clippings. The photograph, which you can see on the cover of this book, must have been taken in Syracuse shortly after they were married, and that picture is one of which dreams are made and stories told. Both were looking directly at the camera and looked so young and innocent. Philip was wearing his "Doughboy" uniform, and Doris was fashionably attired, complete with a wide-brimmed hat and high-heeled boots. Looking at that picture made me want to learn more about them. I also found a newspaper article reporting Philip's admission to the Onondaga County Tuberculosis Sanatorium in 1921 and a few other obituaries. I decided that their story needed to be told. I didn't want them to be forgotten; therefore, I set out to find what else I could learn about them.

I found their birth, death, and marriage certificates and then searched www.ancestry.com and Newspaper Archives for mention of their names. I knew that Philip had grown up in Marshall, Michigan, and I found several articles about him. One reported that he had received a football award, and another reported of his arrangements to enter the Michigan Normal College for the "Business and Shorthand Departments" in August 1916. I did an internet search and found that the school eventually became part of Central Michigan College, Mt. Pleasant, Michigan. Another article reported on February 15, 1919, that Mr. And Mrs. Philip Boughton had visited Mr. and Mrs. Claude Osborn and also "spent the day" in Battle Creek. A report was received in December 1922 that "Mr. Philip Boughton, a former resident of this city, was critically ill at his home in Syracuse and was suffering from ulcers of the lungs." The report stated that his brother, Charles, was with him.

I found fewer articles in the Syracuse Newspapers but did find an account of Doris's arrest at age 14 for causing trouble in the neighborhood after being let off with a warning. There was also a report in August 1918 of Philip being wounded in a battle where he was taken to Base Hospital No. 27 and remained for three weeks.

I learned where the families lived from census records. Among them was a listing for the Bowmans in 1900 where they lived on Elmwood Park Circle, located in the park, with Horace listed as a "Park Attendant," along with Louise and 10-month-old Doris.

I found obituaries from Charlie Boughton, Doris, and Horace and Louise Bowman. Horace died in 1930 after leaving a downtown conference with several attorneys, where he suffered a fatal heart attack. Louise died two years later, no cause given. There was an account of their house being sold for unpaid taxes sometime after Louise's death, so it appears that they were having financial difficulties (the 1929 stock market crash?). My mother had told me the name of Doris's second husband and I was able to find his obituary. He died in the VA hospital in 1960 at the age of 66. He retired from the Syracuse Fire Department and was survived by his widow and several siblings. No children were listed and there was no mention of his first marriage. I located Doris's grave in the Onondaga Valley Cemetery, marked with a simple stone. The caretaker pointed out the spot where Horace and Louise lay nearby in unmarked graves.

William Braun was a real person, although I did change his name in the book from another German name. Most of the details about him are fictional. I know nothing about him other than that he married Doris not long after Philip died. As far as I know, he never worked at Smith Premier or even knew Philip. All other characters are themselves fictional. The names A.L. Wise and Helen Shore are listed as witnesses on Philip's and Doris's marriage certificate, but nothing is known about either, and they are purely fictional characters. A.L. Wise became Philip's Army buddy, Andy Wise, and Helen Shore, Doris's lifelong friend. Dr. LeRoy Hollis was a real person and is well known as the first superintendent of the Oswego County Sanatorium. He modeled the hospital after the famous Trudeau Institute in Saranac Lake and later started a camp for children on the shores of Lake Ontario. Dr. Hollis did sign Philip's death certificate. All other doctors and nurses are fictional.

I visited the places that were part of Philip and Doris's lives. I found the Bowmans' house on Armstrong Avenue, but the little house where Philip and Doris lived on Edgewood Avenue was gone. Elmwood Park is now a city park. I visited the Onondaga Historical Society for more information about it and saw photographs and articles about what the park must have once looked like then.

Among other articles, I read "Elmwood Park – A West Side Gem" by Karen Y. Cooney from the Onondaga Historical Society.

I visited the Methodist Church in the village of Liverpool – now known as "the church with the purple doors." Church historian Sue Slenker gave me a tour of the church and showed me old pictures of what it must have looked like in Philip and Doris's day, with the streetcar tracks running outside the front door and a picture of Reverend Benson. She also showed me the registration they had signed and said that the ceremony probably took place in the parsonage.

The Cobblestone Inn was nearby and I decided that would make a perfect place to have their wedding supper. I called Liverpool Historian Dorianne Gutierrez, and she told me that the inn was built during the salt-making days. She told me about a 1915 ad saying Sunday dinners were a specialty. I also did some internet research and found that, at one time, it was known as The National Hotel. I was unable to determine at what point the names were changed, so I used my artistic license and decided to keep the name The Cobblestone Inn as it had a more romantic sound. Also, during our dating days, my husband, Charlie, and I once had drinks there in the bar. The restaurant is still a popular place to eat and drink. Charlie and I had supper there recently during a visit with my sister and her husband. The walls are now lined with flat-screen televisions, and one can enjoy burgers, pizza, and chicken wings.

I found pictures and stories about what Syracuse looked like in the early nineteen tens and twenties. I saw pictures of downtown as the bustling city that it was, the tracks and streetcars running down the streets. Other articles I found were:

"Closing time at Schrafft's" by Robert Searing about the famous downtown cafe in <u>The Syracuse Post Standard January 5, 2020</u>

"Today in History: Salina Street Reopened to Traffic" about the closing of the Erie Canal from the Onondaga Historical Society

"Syracuse: The Typewriter City" about the Smith Premier Typewriter Company, which eventually became the Smith-Corona Company. <u>The Syracuse Post Standard 2021</u>

"Today in History: Prohibition and Syracuse" from the Onondaga Historical Society

<u>The Golden Age of Onondaga Lake Resorts</u> by Donald Thompson

<u>Syracuse – Images of America</u> Onondaga Historical Society by Dennis Connors

Of course, I found a wealth of information on Wikipedia.

From the internet, I found "<u>thezealoushistorian Syracuse Department Stores in the 20th Century</u>"

I found a whole file about Camp Syracuse, the recruit camp where Philip trained on the grounds of the New York State Fair. I saw many pictures and articles about the camp at the Onondaga Historical Society and visited the museum at the Solvay-Geddes Historical Society, the former site of the camp. I was given a tour by Susan Millet who gave me a wealth of information about the camp.

I also found an article reprinted in the 2021 <u>The Syracuse Post Standard</u> "Camp Syracuse: Answering the Call to Duty."

I made two visits to Marshall, Michigan, the town where I once lived for five years. I had known Nellie Osborn, my great-grandmother, only briefly, but my family and I lived with Claude Osborn for five years in the same house where Philip spent several years on South Marshall Ave. I wrote my 2023 memoir, *Life in Marshall*, based on memories of the town. I visited the Calhoun County Vital Records and the Marshall Public Library, which has a nice local history department. I also found Philip's grave in the Boughton family plot.

I found old photographs of the town *Marshall – Images of America* by Susan Collins and Jane Ammeson in cooperation with the Marshall Historical Society and *Marshall* by Debbie Pardoe and Susan Collins.

I wrote to the Military Personnel Records Center in St. Louis in an attempt to obtain information about Philip's Army record, but I received a reply that those records were destroyed in a 1973 fire. His discharge document reported that he was a Private 1st Class and belonged to Co. H Sixteenth Infantry. The battles in which he took part were also listed, and I read what I could find about those battles and World War I in general. While I could never know the exact circumstances of what actually happened, I tried to place Philip as part of the action in the battles that occurred.

I read *The Last of the Doughboys: The Forgotten Generation and Their Forgotten World War* by Richard Rubin. Written in 2003, Mr. Rubin conducted dozens of interviews with men and women who served in World War I. Reading of their experiences and what it was like to be part of that terrible war helped make it more real to me.

I discovered an internet site: "The Doughboy Center" on *Worldwar1.com*

On this site, I found many articles listing the battles and a wealth of other information.

Among the articles I found were:

"WWI: Life on the Western Front" by Les Jenson

"The Battle of Cantigny and the Dawn of the Modern Army" by Paul Herbert

"American Soldiers Arrive in France" by Chris Kempshall

"The 1st Division: Training and First Battles " – author unknown

"The Battle of Soissons" – author unknown

"St. Mihiel: The Birth of an American Army" by Donald Smith

"Gas: The Greatest Terror of the Great War" by A.P. Padley

"Meuse-Argonne Offensive – 16th Infantry Regiment" by Frederick Castier

I had planned a trip to France in 2020 where I was to visit a tour of the Argonne-Meuse battle site given by Murielle and Frederick Castier. The route would have taken us through the place where Philip had fought and where he was gassed. Unfortunately, that trip had to be canceled due to COVID. I wrote to M. Castier, and he very kindly sent me a detailed description of the route taken by Company H Sixteenth Infantry on October 4th to 9th, where the troops were "inflicted by a heavy mustard gas bombardment," causing 192 casualties. He included a map of the route and photos of the little village of Fleville.

I also found photos on "The Doughboys Center" website with photos and description of Base Hospital 50, Mesves in the south of France where he may have been transported to "receive the fresh air treatment."

Both Philip and Doris died from tuberculosis, a disease that dates from biblical times and earlier. Often called other names like Consumption and The White Plague, no successful treatment was found until the age of antibiotics, mid-20th century. The sanatorium movement started in the nineteenth century in Europe and then spread to this country. I studied the history I learned through the internet. I also visited the Onondaga Historical Society and the Orwell Public Library. Among the articles I used to write the book were:

"Syracuse Area Hospitals – A History of Onondaga County Sanatorium" <u>Health Sciences Library</u>

"Oswego County Sanatorium" <u>Orwell Remembered</u> compiled by Betty D. Martin, Town Historian 1976

"A forgotten arch, stairway to memory: Life at the Old Sanatorium" by Sean Kirst, syracuse.com 2008

I know from my reading that the patients sent there lived in isolation, shut away from families and friends. Visitors were not allowed. A report from a child who had visited her mother at the Orwell Sanatorium said, "We had to talk to her through a screen door." Patients spent much of their time with the windows open regardless of the weather. If able, they were encouraged to walk outside on the grounds to "expand their lungs" but often spent much of the time on bed rest.

According to a newspaper article, Philip was admitted to Onondaga County Sanatorium in 1921 when he was 23. His death certificate from the Oswego County Sanatorium reported his admission from September 1923 to his death in June 1925. What led to him being admitted to both facilities is unknown. The patient records from both hospitals don't seem to exist. Both the Onondaga Health Department and the Onondaga Historical Society had no knowledge of them. I called Oswego County historian Debra Allen, who gave me some information, but she didn't know where the records were. She referred me to the Oswego Records Center but they had no knowledge of the location of those records. I was given other names but to no avail. I have no doubt that there are computerized records somewhere in Albany, New York, the state capital, but it would probably be difficult, if not impossible, to access them. I tried to learn as much as I could about what life was like in a sanatorium.

I read *Open Window: The Lake Julia TB Sanatorium, A Community Created by Tuberculosis* by Pat Nelson 2020, a true account of life at a Sanatorium in Minnesota.

Charlie and I visited the sites of both the local sanatoriums. The Onondaga Sanatorium was torn down years ago, but we found the stone arch still standing in St. Agnes cemetery, bearing the words Onondaga Sanatorium. We walked under the arch and up the broken stone steps that lead to the grounds of the old hospital. We also made a trip to the Orwell Sanatorium where we found the buildings still intact. The facility, now called Unity Acres, is a home for alcoholic men, started by Father McVey. We walked around the grounds, and an employee pointed out where porches once were attached to the windows.

I have spent eight years writing this book, and I hope my words have given meaning to Philip's and Doris's lives. I would like to thank all the people who helped me along the way. A special thank you goes out to my daughter Kathy Warren who proofread all my drafts, and to the team at Wildebeest. My love and gratitude go out to my husband, Charlie Gowing, who was there with me every step of the way. He helped me with research, went to all places we visited, and answered my many computer and technical questions. I never could have done it without him.

ABOUT THE AUTHOR

Author Sandra Gowing was sorting through memorabilia after the loss of her parents. Among the items she found was a photograph of a beautiful couple, whom she learned were her grandparents, Philip and Doris Boughton.

Feeling inspired and not wanting their legacy to be forgotten, Sandra set off on an eight-year research project exploring many books, articles, websites, and landmarks to learn more about the world in which they lived. Her dedication resulted in this fictional love story surrounded by historical facts set in World War I.

Sandra lives in Syracuse, New York, with her loving husband, Charlie. They enjoy traveling, volunteering in the community, and spending time with their children and grandchildren.

Her debut book, *Life in Marshall,* chronicles her charming adventures growing up in Michigan.

9 781958 233313